ACT OF
MERCY

ACT OF MERCY

A DOC BRADY MYSTERY

John Bishop, MD

MANTID PRESS

Act of Mercy

A Doc Brady Mystery

Copyright © 2023 by John Bishop. All rights reserved.
ISBN: 979-8-9861596-5-2 (paperback)
ISBN: 979-8-9861596-6-9 (eBook)
ISBN: 979-8-9861596-7-6 (hardback)
Published by Mantid Press

For information about this title, contact:
Attention: Permissions Department
legalquestions@codedenver.com

CONTENTS

CHAPTER 1

HILL COUNTRY MEDICAL CENTER

I entered the lobby of the Hill Country Medical Center through automatic sliding glass doors; at least, they looked like glass to me. Could have been Plexiglas or some sort of artificial glass that was advertised to be unbreakable or break resistant. I wondered, with wheelchairs and walkers and probably stretchers passing through those doors daily, if they weren't a potential hazard in case of forceful contact. Glass everywhere, cuts and lacerations of a patient or visitor . . . that could get ugly. Although, in that beautiful small Hill Country town called Granite Falls, perhaps the mental wiring of individuals was different from that which I experienced living and practicing orthopedic surgery in Houston for thirty years. Maybe "lawsuit" wasn't the first thing that came to a patient's or victim's mind out here when they were injured. I'm sure I would find out eventually how things worked and how people reacted in this town, but for today, I was definitely overthinking the situation. All over a sliding glass door. But then maybe I was just too well-rested, and my mind was running wind sprints.

Granite Falls was near the junction of Texas Highway 281, which spanned the continental United States north to south from the Canadian border in North Dakota all the way down to the Mexican border in the Rio Grande Valley, and Texas Highway 71, which ran in an east–west direction for a relatively short distance of 250 miles. It was in the Texas Hill Country, an area of Central and West Texas noted for . . . well, hills. The Hill Country contained twenty-five counties plus the metropolitan areas of Austin and San Antonio. The geography was shaped by the dissolving of water-soluble rocks, especially granite and limestone. The topography was also influenced by the Llano Uplift, which included the second-largest granite dome in the US.

These geological formations were noted in the names of counties and towns in the Hill Country: Limestone County, Granite Falls, Marble Falls, Highland Haven, and the town of Llano, to name a few. The Highland Lakes complex also influenced the area, starting with a series of dams along the Colorado River that created Lake Buchanan, Lake LBJ, Lake Marble Falls, Lake Travis, and Lake Austin. The counties and towns of Horseshoe Bay, Cottonwood Shores, and Granite Shoals were likewise named for the various bodies of water created by the construction of the Granite Shoals Dam by the Lower Colorado River Authority in 1950.

All this geography and geology, created over millions of years of planetary construction combined with more-recent engineering by humanity, resulted in a spectacular blend of rolling hills and lakes, with a mild climate and relatively low humidity. Not to say it didn't get cold in the winter, and yes there was heat in the summer, but it was a spectacular place to live. Which is why I found myself at Hill Country Medical Center, sitting in the midst of all this Texas beauty.

There was a security desk in front of a wall in the middle of the entry corridor. I introduced myself to the guard sitting there. He referred to a clipboard and gave me a nod. "Dr. Brady, welcome to Hill Country Medical Center. Dr. Owens's office is down the hall to your left. Have a good day, sir."

I followed the hallway as instructed and said good morning to the receptionist at a semicircular desk adjacent to the administrative offices. "I'm Dr. Jim Bob Brady. I have an appointment with Dr. Owens?"

The nameplate at the desk she was occupying read Lucinda Williams. She stood, shook my hand, and asked if I needed a beverage other than the coffee, water, and sodas that were set up in the conference room.

"That sounds fine to me. Is your mother a fan? Of Lucinda Williams?"

"Oh, yes, that's about all I heard, growing up. Country, blues, rock, and folk all rolled into one strong husky voice. Just call me Lucy, please."

She was medium height, trim, cute like you'd see in a *Good Housekeeping* feature. Her brown hair was trimmed in sort of a pixie style. She had on a nurse's scrub uniform, with loose-fitting pants and pullover top all in blue. What I noticed most was a left black eye. She seemed to have a look of melancholy about her. Why I thought that, I'm not sure. I had a myriad of patients over the years with all sorts of orthopedic problems, but I could never isolate those problems away from personality issues in my clientele. I could spot a depressed patient, that's for certain.

"How's the other fellow?" I asked.

"Excuse me?"

"The black eye."

"Oh, that. I was squatting down at home, trying to retrieve a chafing dish from under the counter, and slammed my forehead on the edge of a cabinet door. The doctors X-rayed it, said nothing was broken and my eye wasn't damaged. It doesn't really hurt any longer; it's just the subject of conversation."

Lucinda Williams did not know me, nor I her, but I have a sixth sense regarding mysterious occurrences, what my wife Mary Louise calls pernicious meddling. I was immediately suspicious about her black eye, and her explanation for the temporary disfigurement would not hold water. Had she known me better, I might have shared some of my experiences over the years in dealing with miscreants and their heinous deeds, but I thought better of it, and kept my suspicions to myself for the time being.

She changed the subject quickly and said, "Let me show you the conference room, Dr. Brady. I also function as Dr. Owens's administrative assistant, so if you are in need of something, please let me know."

The interior of the facility was beautiful, with walls of white limestone, plentiful in the Hill Country of Texas. The floors were of a matching color in some sort of durable ceramic tile. The ceiling was very high, with fans rotating slowly. There was a time when fans were not allowed in clinical areas due to the supposed risk of increased infections, but that had been debunked. In warm climates and summer seasons, fans were essential for adequate ventilation.

I noticed signs for radiology, MRI and CT scanning, laboratory, emergency room, an urgent-care center, and outpatient chemotherapy. The building had three stories, and I assumed for the moment that the operating rooms, recovery rooms, and ICUs were on the second floor. The third floor was more than likely hospital beds and nursing stations. Having been working in twenty-five-story buildings for most of my training and career, this facility seemed to have all the right divisions, just on a much smaller scale.

Lucy escorted me into a conference room with a mahogany table surrounded by eight comfortable chairs with a purple print pattern on the seats and backs. The fellow at the head of the table stood and introduced himself.

"I'm Buck Owens, Dr. Brady. Pleasure to meet you. Welcome to HCMC."

He was somewhat shorter than me, with a tanned and lined face and a full head of gray hair.

"Please, call me Jim or Jim Bob. Seems I am in the presence of music royalty today. A Buck Owens and a Lucinda Williams."

He laughed. "My given name is Royal Owens, which was my mother's family name. I'm a little older than you, but you may remember that naming children in the old days was about making a tribute to relatives long passed or creating nicknames that ascribed certain traits of an individual."

"Oh yes, I had eight aunts and uncles on my dad's side and eight on my mother's side, and each and every one had a given name and a nickname. With their spouses, that made thirty different names to remember at the family reunions. And the names weren't easy, they were like Tinkum for Lyla, Dude for Gladys, and Girlie for Margaret. Crazy stuff. I finally gave up, just called my older relatives ma'am and sir."

"So you can understand why I finally had folks call me Buck. A name like 'Royal' got your butt kicked when I was growing up in Weatherford, Texas, but 'Buck' got me a free pass. At any rate, I'm happy to have you here today. You'll meet some other folks a little later. Tell me a little about yourself, if you don't mind. I obviously have your bio here, but I'd like to hear you tell your story in your own words."

"I grew up in Waco, went to Baylor undergraduate school. Then I went down to Houston, graduated from Baylor med school, and did my internship and orthopedic surgery residency at the University Hospitals. After that training was done, I did a hip and knee replacement fellowship at Special Surgery in New York, then returned to Houston and joined the University Orthopedic Group, part of the University Hospital complex. I served as a clinician and a professor of orthopedic surgery there for almost thirty years. Now I'm on a three-month sabbatical, sort of a retirement trial run, trying to find my niche in life. I've been spending the first month here in the Hill Country. I have the option to return to my old job after the sabbatical, and after all this looking around, maybe I'll do just that. But for now, I am actively seeking a new environment of some sort. And I'm not even sure what that is supposed to be. And it may not involve being an orthopedic surgeon any longer, although as far as I can tell, I have limited other skills."

"It's nice to have the luxury of finding yourself without having to worry about making a living at the same time. I understand a few years ago you came into a . . . shall we say, financial windfall?"

"Yes. How in the world would you know about that?"

"Harold Sanders was an old friend of mine from the University of Texas days and the oil patch days. I've kept in touch with the family. I happened to be on the hunting trip when he was shot."

Mr. Harold Sanders was chair of the University Hospital board and a prominent Houston citizen and oil wildcatter. He had been shot in the leg during opening weekend of spring turkey season many years prior by a colleague, and he eventually died of diabetic-related complications. In his will, he had left me one hundred acres of land in Cotulla, in South Texas, which turned out to be chock full of oil and natural gas. After the discovery, his wife and sons bought me out of the property, and I ended up with over $16 million dollars free and clear of taxes and legal fees. That windfall has produced an income that was three times what I had been taking home after taxes and expenses as a surgeon working fifty to seventy hours per week.

"Wow, what a small world. But your 'oil patch days'? I thought you were an MD. Lucy introduced you as Dr. Owens."

"I was a family doc for many years but invested in the oil business through some old college buddies of mine, one of which was Harold Sanders. We got lucky on a few wells in the Permian Basin, which set me up for life. I eventually retired from patient care and found my calling in the hospital administration business. With some wealthy and generous benefactors, we established this medical center several years back. We have outlying clinics in Burnet, Llano, Brady, and Georgetown, and several more in the wings, all feeding patients down here. I've found that there are many other ways to treat patients and influence the course of an individual's health care besides being on the front lines of medicine. Of course, we need those patient-care doctors as well, but I was able to change directions in my life, much as it sounds like the situation you've found yourself in. The biggest problem I had to overcome was the guilt."

"Guilt? About what, abandoning your training and direct patient care? I'm already losing sleep over it and I'm only one month into the sabbatical."

Buck laughed. "See, that insidious guilt has already crept in and found you. That's the way we docs are engineered, feeling that direct patient care is the only avenue to justify all that training. But I'm telling you, Jim Bob, there are many other ways to stay involved in medicine and help folks. You don't have to worry about forsaking the Hippocratic oath. You'll find your niche, just wait and see.

"In case you were wondering how I came into contact with you and asked you to come over and visit with us, it was through the Sanders family. They heard we were looking for another orthopedic surgeon with a hip and knee subspecialty, and although

Mrs. Sanders passed away a few years back, the sons remembered you well. The family recommended you for consideration here at HCMC, thinking you might be interested in a change of scenery, now that you and your wife had become financially independent. One of Harold's sons serves on our board."

"That answers the questions we had about the contact. It came unexpectedly through a headhunter, a firm that I had not even been in touch with. It seemed odd at the time, but since Mary Louise and I had leased an apartment on the water here at Horseshoe Bay Resort for a month, and we were playing golf almost every day, we were obviously familiar with the area. We thought it mighty coincidental to hear about a potential job opportunity in an area that where we were staying—and falling in love with, by the way."

"Where is your wife?"

"She's meeting me. I believe she had a date with the hair stylist. She should be here any moment."

"Then let's get that tour going, shall we?"

CHAPTER 2

THE TOUR

As we stood, the conference room door opened and Lucy Williams entered, followed closely by Mary Louise Brady, my bride of thirty-seven years. She was dressed in peach-colored pants, open-toed white heels that showcased painted toenails that matched her pants, and a white silk blouse that revealed just enough cleavage to make life interesting. Her long blond hair was done up in some sort of twist, with thin ribbons of bangs. All in all, quite the package, the sight of which stirred my bad self into suggesting silently the tour be abandoned posthaste.

"Mary Louise Brady," she said to Buck, who apparently was charmed speechless by the arrival of my wife. She shook his hand, then turned to me and gave me an air kiss on each side of my face. "I hope I didn't miss anything of great importance."

"Not at all, Mrs. Brady. We're just about to take a tour of the facilities," Buck sputtered.

"Wonderful. And please call me Mary Louise," she said, taking my arm and squeezing her ample chest into my flesh. And then she winked at me. Cruel woman, this one.

"How did you get here?" I whispered. We had only one car there.

"Lyft," she replied.

We browsed the facilities on the first floor that had the signs I had noticed upon arrival announcing their presence, as well as physical therapy, occupational therapy, and a Wellness Center located in an adjacent concourse. The facility seemed massive.

"We have about 100,000 square feet of space on each of the three floors," Buck said. "We're using most of the space on this floor for all of our ancillary services. The Wellness Center area is not completed, but we hope to have that up and running in the next few months. A Wellness Center is a popular term these days, but best I can tell, it's the same sort of concept as having a yearly physical but with much better advertising. Preventative medicine and all that is quite the rage these days."

We stepped to the elevator bank and shortly thereafter had a quiet ride to the second floor. The door opened into a large waiting area. There were a few dozen folks sitting there, and I noticed a veritable cornucopia of crutches, walkers, and braces. I assumed this was the pre- and post-op waiting area. A large desk lay in the center of the room, staffed by what appeared to be volunteers. I gleaned that from the nametags they wore, that read VOLUNTEER. They both stood upon our arrival.

"Dr. Owens, good morning," both women said.

"Morning, ladies. Please say hello to Dr. and Mrs. Brady. Dr. Brady is considering coming to work here at HCMC."

"Oh my, Dr. Brady," said one volunteer. "This is such a wonderful institution, and they do so much good work for the community. You would just love it here, I'm sure."

I didn't know I was here on a job interview. I was here, at least in my opinion, to look at options for what I wanted to do with my life. Working here on a much smaller scale than I had in the past was one of those options. But so was collecting my monthly investment income and laying on a beach somewhere, drinking brightly colored drinks with little umbrellas at ten in the morning. I was near the end of the first month of my sabbatical, and I regret to admit that standing here in another hospital almost made me break out in a cold sweat. Most likely, the thought of seeing all those patients waiting in the surgical waiting room triggered stress anxiety. I definitely was not ready to return to my former work schedule.

"We'll have to tour the actual operating rooms another time. All six rooms are in use today for most of the day, so unless you folks want to change into scrubs, they are off limits for examination. We have room to add four more surgical suites when the timing is appropriate."

I appreciated a wall of windows opposite the surgical admittance desk, with a view of the parking lot and Texas hills beyond. Certainly a serene setting, contrasted by the sea of people in the waiting room with all varieties of medical problems requiring surgical attention. Some of these folks might even be dying, as we calmly toured the facilities. I pondered these lofty metaphysical comparisons until I heard my name called.

"Jim, let's walk through the areas open to inspection," Dr. Buck Owens said. He toured Mary Louise and I through the intake area, where patients were required to disrobe and put on skimpy hospital gowns with the string ties in the back, affixed where, of course, they were unreachable. Following this indignity, the patients had to parade around with their respective asses hanging out while temperatures and blood pressures were taken and identifying wrist bands were applied.

We passed through into the pre-op area, where IVs were started, operative permits were reviewed and signed, and surgeons identified their respective patients and confirmed which particular organ or limb was being operated on. Patients were then wheeled back into the DO NOT ENTER area, which housed the six operating rooms in a large U-shape, according to Buck, my tour guide.

"We have a robotics operating room back there—a Da Vinci system—very useful for procedures such as prostate removal, during which the important nerve fibers necessary for male performance, shall we say, need to be preserved. The system is also ideal for gall bladder removal, gynecological procedures, kidney surgery and such. Robotic procedures reduce blood loss and postoperative pain by using smaller incisions and more precise operating techniques, which in turn produces faster recoveries."

He sounded like a salesman for the robotics manufacturer. I had no personal experience with robotic surgery, since there was minimal use for those techniques in orthopedic surgery. But I could see that perhaps in the future, the use of robotics in hip and knee replacements might have a role, what with the need for precision in the bone-cutting process and subsequent insertion of implants. For now, however, most of my colleagues felt they could make a cut with a bone saw as good as a machine.

The next station was the post-op area, where recovering patients slowly awakened and were put on the runway toward home or were ultimately shuffled into an elevator and hustled upstairs onto the third floor, where the hospital rooms were.

"We have sixty beds at this time, expandable to one hundred as our needs change over time," said Buck. "Do you folks want to see the top floor?"

I'd been staring at Mary Louise's backside for a while now, and I wanted to scream NO and streak back to the apartment for some quality time. So, when she answered, "Certainly, Buck," I felt deflated and temporarily dejected. We boarded another elevator toward floor three, and during the ride Mary Louise stood behind me and surreptitiously rubbed her hand against my butt, so I rekindled my hopes that all was not lost.

The third floor housed the inpatient hospital beds. There was a large waiting room at the entry with a wall of windows facing east. The layout was, like the operating suites, in a giant U, with beds along the west, north, and south walls, and a massive nursing station in the center.

"The architects designed the floor plan to house twenty rooms on each side. If patient volume increases at the same rate since opening, we'll need to expand in the next three to five years. We'll have to get a certificate of need from the state, but that wasn't a problem when we built the facility and shouldn't be a problem in the future. The closest Level I facility to us is in south Austin, and with the current populations of our primary draw area—Burnet County, Llano County, and Kingsland County—continually rising, that's 80,000 people we're serving now. And that doesn't include all the part-timers from around Texas who have homes here on Lake LBJ, nor the tourists that come in droves to play golf and enjoy the boating activities on the various lakes here. The board calculates that we're currently serving about 100,000 folks at this institution. The medical business here is booming, Jim Bob, and we sure hope you'll become a part of it."

With that, Buck's cell phone jingled. He glanced at the screen and said he was sorry, that he had an emergency to deal with. He would have to reschedule meeting the other officers of HCMC, as well as the tour of the adjacent office building where the physicians had their offices. We rode together back down to the first floor, where Mary Louise and I said goodbye to Lucy Williams and Buck Owens and showed ourselves out.

CHAPTER 3

CONFUSION AND INDECISION

I woke up amidst tangled sheets, a little groggy and unsure of my location. I stood, glanced at the deck, saw the crystal-clear blue waters of Lake LBJ, and got my bearings. After the HCMC tour, we had gone over to a diner named the Hole in One and gorged ourselves on fried catfish, fried shrimp, fried oysters, fried okra, and steak fries, washing it all down with a pitcher of light beer, as if that single action would mitigate the carb loading. Lunch had been followed by an exuberant romp in the hay, and shortly thereafter, an afternoon siesta for the Bradys.

We had rented a beautiful apartment on the sixth and top floor of a condominium complex that sat steps away from Lake LBJ. The main buildings of Hill Country Resort were nearby, and from my vantage point I noticed in the distance a large number of white chairs set up adjacent to a gazebo, probably for a wedding later in the evening. We had been here three and a half weeks and had enjoyed a number of free concerts from our deck.

Tip, our golden retriever, was still asleep next to Mary Louise, so I quietly crept into the kitchen and tried to rehydrate with a bottle of Smart Water. I went outside, sat on the deck, and pondered my situation. We still had our high-rise apartment in Houston, and when I decided to take a sabbatical, I was in good stead with the University Orthopedic Group. I had met with my old friend Dr. Greg Mayfield, now chief operating officer of the group, and a busy spine surgeon to boot. Most of my colleagues who had heard of our windfall some years back were completely understanding of my need to take a step back and look at my life introspectively. I think most were more than envious of my ability to do that. It's difficult to see what your life is really like when you're in the midst of it, what with working long hours and putting your patients above yourself, which is what the majority of dedicated physicians do.

After thirty long years in practice, not counting the four years of med school and six years of surgical training, I felt confident that I had helped a helluva lot of people. If I had hurt or injured someone along the way, I didn't know about it, and couldn't have stood that. And I could have continued to go along as in the past, seeing patients, operating on those that needed indicated procedures, and basically not changing my life at all. However, I'm embarrassed to say that I felt differently about my job, knowing that I really didn't have to do it any longer. I was racked with guilt, though, about my hesitation to adhere to my unspoken duties and continue to take care of patients and give it my all, as I had these many years. But I kept coming back to the possibility that if I didn't have to do it anymore, I might not want to. When was "giving it all you had" enough? And knowing myself, with all that training and experience, what would make me feel like a still-worthy individual if I no longer was involved in direct patient care?

I was startled by the sense of a wet tongue on my hand, and there was Tip, my faithful dog, wagging his tail, making me forget all about my worries for a moment, life coming down in reality to something as simple as *what would Tip like to eat for dinner???* We padded into the kitchen and I dished up his regular canine food.

But then, because he was such a good boy, I cut up a few pieces of leftover ribeye steak from the prior night's dinner, mixed it in with his food, and served that to him. He took a couple of bites, looked up at me, licked his lips and, I swear, smiled. And I wondered, who's taking care of whom in this relationship?

I took him downstairs for a walk. On the elevator, we encountered a fellow going down to walk his dog, a cute little female Lhasa Apso with a couple of pink ribbons in her hair. She was very excited to meet Tip, and the two dogs did the usual sniff and retreat routine. When we reached the ground floor, we went our separate ways so that our pets could get to their business. Tip looked back at his new friend as we headed to the dog park and barked a soft "ruff."

"How was the walk?" asked Mary Louise when we returned, now up and dressed in a thick terry-cloth robe, sitting on the deck in the waning sunlight. I took the chair next to her and removed Tip's leash.

"Great. We met a new friend in the elevator, a cute female Lhasa. I think Tip has a crush."

"And how are you doing?"

"Good. Fine. Excellent."

"No, I mean how are you really doing?"

"Man, I don't know. Torn by guilt, wanting to be excited about new possibilities, but afraid to leave the past behind. Confused about what I want to do versus what I feel obligated to do."

"Remember, Buck told you there are a lot of ways to help people other than direct patient care. He was in your situation at one time. I think you need time to sort those issues out, and I seriously doubt you can do it while working your old schedule at University Medical Center. You might be able to find yourself and sort things out working an abbreviated schedule somewhere else, like maybe at HCMC, but you might just need to take the allotted three months off to figure it out. I'm here for you any way you want to go about it, but from my angle, you need some time to get your wits about you. Tip and I are here to provide you emotional and physical support. Your life. Your time. Your decision. And remember, we'll love you regardless of what you decide to do.

"And I want you to enjoy this windfall you've received, whether through fate, kismet, or some sort of cosmic reward for a job well done. You have barely touched the interest on the principal, choosing to continue working full steam for the most part for the several years since you received the inheritance. Most of all, I want you to be happy."

At the end of the one-month apartment rental period, we returned to Houston. I needed to get back and go to the office to sign charts. Even though I was currently not seeing patients or operating, there was a backlog of charts in medical records that had to be completed. Joint Commission rules and all. I went there early in the morning the day after our return. I didn't particularly want to see my friends and colleagues, since I was in a different world than they were. Time had passed. I was free to do whatever I wanted; they were not. I didn't want to have any more discussions about my long-term plans.

My two personal employees—my nurse Rita and my administrative assistant Franny—had been farmed out to other doctors. They were happy to still be working at the University Orthopedic Clinic, with ample time off for holidays and excellent health insurance. My existing patients had been absorbed by other physicians in the group, as had new patients that were calling to schedule appointments. My practice that I had worked so long and hard for was already cast to the winds of change, now the responsibility of my colleagues. My mail was being collected by the clinic

administrator, who had kindly left the packet on my desk. Also, all
the hospital charts requiring discharge summaries or my signature
were on my desk. It took me an hour to dictate and sign off on the
charts and go through the mail, most of which was medical "junk."
I had arrived at 6 a.m. and was out the door by 7:30 a.m. I took
an indirect route out of the office, wandered to the freight elevator, and rode the twenty-one floors down into the parking garage
without seeing a single physician or employee of the clinic, or anyone else for that matter except the security guard. He regretted
to inform me that my parking pass was being nullified that day,
and my space was being assigned to another orthopedic surgeon.
I had spent thirty years in the University Orthopedic Clinic and
the University Hospital System, with ten years of training prior
to that, and I was sneaking out of the building like a bandit in the
night with not so much as a parking pass.

I was in a different place and time in my life.

CHAPTER 4

LUCY WILLIAMS

After being gone for a month and eating all sorts of terrible things, as we did on our fried-food rampage, we decided to cook in and eat reasonably healthily. The waistline of my jeans felt pretty tight, so I needed to lose a few pounds. Mary Louise was in the same boat.

So, we prepared baked chicken, a salad, and green beans and asparagus, and opened a bottle of cold pinot grigio, which we sipped while we cooked. The wine was so good, we finished it during the preparation process, requiring me to open a fresh bottle for dinner. At that point, Mary Louise mentioned that perhaps pinot grigio and all the other varieties of alcohol we had imbibed over the past month might be a source of the weight-gain problem. Being a physician, and having special knowledge in the matters of metabolism, I allowed as how that was preposterous. All that fried food we had eaten was the culprit. We could continue with our usual selection of beverages and simply change our eating habits. No problem, I assured her . . . but wondered if she were correct. I certainly hoped not.

After we washed the dishes and cleaned up the kitchen, we sat down to watch another installment of a top television show that was now several years old but that we had missed due to my intense work schedule. It was called *Breaking Bad*, about a high school chemistry teacher short on funds who becomes a producer of high quality methamphetamine, and all the trials and tribulations that go along with being a drug maker and, eventually, drug dealer. I especially enjoyed these new TV apps that provided a commercial-free viewing experience.

My cell phone rang, and I paused the program and looked at the number.

"This looks like an Austin-area number. Think it's a robocall?" I asked Mary Louise.

"No idea. Didn't you get a blocking app for your phone?"

"I think so." So, I pressed the ANSWER icon. "Dr. Brady," I said, out of habit from the good old days.

"Dr. Brady, I'm so embarrassed to bother you this evening, but I'm in trouble and I need your help."

"I'm sorry, but who is this?"

"Lucy Williams, from Hill Country Medical Center. I got your cell number from the paperwork you sent Dr. Owens prior to your visit with us."

"Okay. What kind of problem can I help you with, and why would you be calling me? We just met a few days ago, and only spoke for—"

"My daughter, Julie Bates, is here in the emergency room at HCMC. She was run over by a car and has a broken hip, a fractured pelvis, and a broken forearm bone, I forget which one. I need you to take care of her."

"Lucy, I can appreciate your concern for your daughter, but I live in Houston, and I'm not a member of the hospital staff there. There are, as I understand, several quality orthopedic surgeons that work at HCMC, who I'm sure are nearby and available to take of your daughter's injuries. I'm sorry, but I'm not your man for the job."

"Dr. Welker came and saw her and reviewed the X-rays. He said the pelvic fracture is not operable and will have to heal in traction and bedrest over time. He can fix the forearm fracture, but he said he doesn't know what to do with the hip. It's fractured in an unusual location, and he wants to transfer her over to Austin via ambulance. You're a hip specialist and I'm sure you would know what to do. I don't want her to have to leave here, and I'm hoping you would be able to come over and repair the hip for us."

I was speechless for a moment, looked at Mary Louise, and didn't know what to say or do. She probably had the gist of the what I was being asked to do from listening to my side of the conversation. She raised her eyebrows and nodded, and I knew by her facial expression that I was about to go and do something I really didn't want to do.

Lucy spoke again. "Dr. Owens has granted you full staff privileges and has approved you to come over and take care of her hip problem. He also had an emergency rider attached to HCMC's malpractice policy, granting you immunity from legal entanglements, sort of like the Good Samaritan law. I am begging you, Dr. Brady."

"Lucy, it's late, I've had some wine this evening, and it's a four-hour drive there, depending on traffic. I cannot get in the car and drive there this evening."

"That's okay. Julie has some medical problems that have to get sorted out, so in the morning will be just fine. We'll keep her NPO for surgery. Thanks so much, Dr. Brady. I knew you would come. And by the way, not that you need to be especially careful or anything, but Julie told me during an alert moment that she and her husband Rob were coming out of the movie in Marble

Falls, saw an oncoming car speeding toward their exit path, and Rob pushed her into the vehicle."

We hung up, and I related the entire story to Mary Louise. "I really don't like what I'm getting myself into. I don't so much mind going over to do the hip surgery—in fact, it's somewhat flattering, after having my parking pass rescinded today—but the part about the husband shoving his wife into the path of an oncoming car? That sounds like trouble to me. And you know how I try and avoid trouble."

"Don't get me wrong, I don't want you to put yourself in any sort of physical danger, but we don't know the facts of the accident. Maybe the daughter is on medication, or had a concussion, and is confused about the facts. I mean, people coming out of a movie, a crowd around, who in their right mind would try and pull off something that seems to me so obvious? I suspect she's mistaken, Jim Bob."

"Well, I hope you're right. Anyway, I need to hit the sack soon if we have to drive back over to Granite Falls early in the morning."

"There will be no 'we,' young man. I have a March of Dimes board meeting, and a Crohn's and Colitis Foundation donor dinner, and my presence at both those functions is required. I'm sorry, but you'll have to make the trip solo, unless you want to take Tip along."

"I don't know, Mary Louise. I expect it to be a short trip, maybe a night or two to make sure the daughter is stabilized. I can't see any reason why I would need to be there longer than that. The pelvic fracture doesn't require surgery, according to Dr. Welker, whomever he is. And Lucy said that he's willing to operate on the forearm fracture while I repair the hip. So I'm just going over like a hired gun to do one thing. And hopefully I can do it. What if it's beyond repair? Then I've wasted their time and mine. Oh, man, I probably shouldn't even go."

"Jim Bob, just calm yourself. All will be fine. I see this experience as one door closing and another opening. I'm proud of you. You're still a wanted man, in more ways than one. Speaking of which, perhaps you should follow me into the boudoir for a little physical therapy, you know, to get you calmed down and sleepy."

"That's an offer that I can't refuse. I'll take Tip downstairs for his last walk."

"You do that, while I . . . prepare myself."

My canine companion and I almost ran to the elevator. I said to Tip, "Make it a fast one, fella."

CHAPTER 5

EMERGENCY ROOM

I awoke at 5 a.m. out of habit. Mary Louise and Tip were still in REM sleep, or so it seemed from the deep breathing sounds coming from each of them. I padded into the bathroom, showered and dressed, and packed a bag for a couple of days' stay in Granite Falls.

I brewed a new coffee blend, Sumatra Gold, a little robust for the morning but an excellent choice to keep me wide awake on the drive. I topped off my to-go cup, peeked in the bedroom to confirm sleep still prevailed there, and headed out. But not before I found a scratch pad and pen in the kitchen, drew a large heart, and signed my name.

Good news was, I was driving against the traffic, most of which was traveling east and south into Houston from outlying communities. My route was west on Richmond, north on Loop 610, and west on Interstate 10, also called the Katy Freeway by locals, because it took you to the town of Katy. I-10 westbound could take you all the way to downtown Los Angeles and the Pacific Ocean, and eastbound to Jacksonville, Florida, and the Atlantic Ocean. And I was just another vehicle moving west on the GPS system, monitored by whom, I did not know. Humbling to think of myself as just another dot . . .

I exited Interstate 10 and traveled west on Texas Highway 71, through the towns of LaGrange, Smithville—my dad's birthplace—Bastrop, and into Austin, where the traffic came to a dead stop. I fumed for a while, moved at a stop-and-go pace, worried that the engine might overheat, then assumed that sort of thing didn't happen in a Chevy Tahoe, unlike my ancient Mercedes SEL sedan, which was more likely than not being used for parts down in Mexico. Once out of the city limits of Austin, there was no traffic on the remainder of the drive into Granite Falls. It took me slightly less than four hours, not bad on a work day. I was starving by then, so I detoured into town and purchased a couple of Sausage McMuffins with Egg in the McDonald's drive-thru and washed them down with really good hot coffee. Breakfast of champions.

I parked in the visitor lot and entered the front lobby as before, after brushing the crumbs off the front of my shirt. I walked to the information desk, and Lucy Williams was there, as she had been a few days ago. She stepped around the desk and gave me a hug. "I'm so glad you agreed to come. Please, let me get my replacement to fill in at the desk, and we'll go to the emergency room and see Julie."

"She's still in the ER?"

"Yes, there were more tests to be run, and the staff knew she would be going to the operating room this morning, so they left her there."

Lucy looked haggard, which was to be expected, and her uniform was wrinkled as though she might have slept in it. Her hair was out of perfect order, and she was pale. I don't know how I would feel if our son J. J. was in her daughter's situation, but more than likely not much different from Lucy.

We walked toward the east end of the building, made a left turn, and entered the massive emergency department. Lucy told me there were twenty-four beds, each a private room. I noticed there were two shock rooms for trauma victims, each equipped with all the necessary items a Level I trauma hospital would require: syringes, cannulas, medications, oxygen masks, defibrillators, intubation laryngoscopes, EKG machines, overhead X-ray tubes . . . the works.

We stopped in a room across from the nursing station. It was quite roomy for an ER room, about twelve by twelve feet. The woman in the bed was sleeping, with IVs in the subclavian vein in her chest and one in her left arm. Her bladder catheter showed clear urine. She was on nasal oxygen and had a splint on her right arm, and her right leg had a small traction device around her ankle with a five-pound weight attached. A hip fracture causes the leg to draw up from muscle spasm, and the weight counteracts that to keep the patient reasonably comfortable prior to surgery. Lucy held her daughter's hand, but there was no verbal response. I might have noticed a slight squeeze from the patient, but that could have been wishful thinking.

"She's got a concussion, Lucy," said a nurse who entered the room. "We did an MRI during the night because her neural responses were slow. There isn't a subdural or epidural hematoma, so no drill holes required, thank the good Lord for that. Are you Dr. Brady? I'm Louann Simms, charge nurse on the seven-to-three shift," she said, shaking my hand. Louann was dressed in green scrub pants and matching shirt, with a stethoscope around her neck. Her hair was hidden by a surgical bonnet, and her face was devoid of makeup. She had a nice smile and might have played basketball or volleyball in her younger days, as she was the same height as me.

"Jim Brady. Pleasure. So she's not sedated? That somnolence is from the head injury?"

"Yes, sir. Her vitals are good, though, so the neurosurgeon doesn't think there will be any residuals. The general surgeon was in this morning. He said that usually there is some internal organ damage from the impact that is bad enough to fracture the pelvis, but she was lucky. The kidneys, spleen, liver, and bladder are all okay. He checked out the MRIs, and there's no blood coming from her Foley catheter."

"Great. Now, Louann, I really need to see the hip and pelvic X-rays. Do you have a viewing room?"

"Yes, sir. Lucy, stay with that child of yours, and I'll take Doc Brady to see the films. You okay, honey?"

Lucy nodded and dabbed her eyes with a tissue.

We walked down the internal corridor, past all those ER beds, mostly full of patients, into a large viewing room. The walls were covered by X-ray boxes. She went to a file box, extracted a wad of films, and brought them to me. "Forearm films, hip and pelvis films, MRIs of the hip, pelvis, and cranium. Want me to put them up for you in sequence?"

"That would be great, Louann. But first, where can I get a cup of coffee? I just made the drive from Houston."

"Black?"

"Yes, but I can get it myself."

"No way. Lucy and I are best friends, and it's the least I can do after you've come all this way. We appreciate you, you know."

She put the films up in expert fashion, then left to get coffee.

I found a notepad and pen and jotted down my findings as I reviewed all the films. Louann entered with coffee, and trailing behind her was a bear of a man dressed in blue scrubs and wearing a long white coat. He had to be six and a half feet tall, and had a shaved head and no facial hair.

"Dick Welker. You the hip man from Houston?"

"Jim Brady. Tell me you were a tight end."

He laughed. "Yep, Texas A&M years ago. Blew out my knee the last game of my senior year. The agent thought I would go in the first round of the draft, but this old knee cut that career short . . . like to a zero-percent chance. So, I finished up my undergrad schooling, went to med school, and now I'm fixing all those injuries we players used to get. See the films yet?"

"Just did. I agree the pelvic fracture is probably nonoperable. What worries me is that on one of the MRI views there is a faint crack into the acetabulum." That's the "cup" part of the pelvis that forms a socket into which the femoral head fits, creating the hip joint. "And that fracture, man, the femoral head is broken into at least four pieces. Was that from the direct impact or from the subsequent fall?"

"We think from the impact. She has a huge ecchymotic area over her hip, much more than a bruise, probably a hematoma. Ever seen a fracture like that?"

"Yes, unfortunately. How old is she?"

"Forty-two," said Nurse Simms.

"I don't think it's repairable," I said. "Considering the nature of the fracture, she probably has disrupted all the blood supply to the femoral head. The pelvis fracture extends into the acetabulum, so it will more than likely take a hip replacement to repair it, with either bone graft or cement infused up into the pelvis area to seat the cup properly so it will house the ball component tightly. Not for the faint of heart, Dick."

"That's why I wanted to send her to Austin. Treating this injury is above my pay grade. I'm happy to fix the radius fracture while you tackle the hip. That'll save her some anesthesia time. I can work with her arm extended ninety degrees. What about you? Anterior or posterior incision?"

"Anterior for sure. I'd like to try and stay out of the pelvic area as much as possible, except for that pesky crack into the acetabulum. Hopefully I can access it all from the front. What's her weight? I couldn't see with her under the covers."

"I'd say 110 pounds, no more. She's a skinny little thing, where I come from, Doc," said Louann.

"That's the best news I've heard since I arrived."

CHAPTER 6

SURGERY

"**H**ow did it go, Dr. Brady?" asked Lucy Williams.

"It went well, considering the extent of the damage. It took about four hours to get the procedures done. Dr. Welker did a nice job of plating her radius fracture. The fragments came together nicely, and the forearm is now stable. She'll have a cast for a couple of weeks, then when the sutures are removed, she can go into a splint and start exercising her fingers and wrist. Long-term, she should be fine.

"The hip fracture was as I feared, only worse. The femoral head was destroyed by the fractures. Unfortunately the pelvic fracture not only extended into the acetabulum, or cup, but strayed horizontally above the acetabulum. We both looked at the MRI during the case and could not see that additional fracture line, but it made the pelvis unstable above the hip joint area. So, I had to put in three screws with washers to hold the pelvic fracture together, then carefully ream out the old acetabulum and insert a new cup with cement not only behind the cup area but for several inches above the cup where the pelvic fracture lines extended. Then I removed the pieces of the head, inserted the new ball with attached stem and cemented all that in place. It's very stable now, but she'll have to keep weight off that leg for at least six weeks.

She'll be on bed rest for at least the next three weeks to allow some time for the pelvic fractures to begin to heal. What's her status, as far as where she'll be?"

Lucy breathed a heavy sigh. "Well, she can stay here at HCMC for the number of days allotted by her insurance company. After that, I'm hoping she'll get approved for a rehab unit. HCMC has one on the third floor, separate from the hospital wing, but with only twelve beds. Otherwise, she'll have to be moved to another facility over in Marble Falls."

"That's only what, ten or fifteen miles from here?"

"Yes, sir, but it's about the care here. It's far superior to all the other facilities in the Hill Country. And here, I can keep an eye on my baby girl."

"I see. Well, I'll put in a good word for you with Dr. Owens if you think that will help."

"It certainly couldn't hurt. Listen, Dr. Brady, I was out of line last night when I told you that Rob, my son-in-law, was responsible for Julie's injury. Truth of the matter, I have no proof of that. Julie was in and out of consciousness due to the injuries, and she was babbling to some extent. Rob has a bit of a temper, so you have to be a little careful when discussing any issue with him that might involve him being at fault. But I did bring it up, and he insists he was trying to pull Julie away from the path of the car, not push her into it. And that does make sense, considering they were exiting a movie and there were lots of other people around."

"Was Julie the only one injured?"

"I believe so. Rob told me they caught the driver a few blocks from the theater. He was a teenager high on PCP and had run his car into a tree. There wasn't a scratch on him, so they took him straight to jail. He'll be charged with attempted murder and leaving the scene of a crime, along with a few other items thrown in, depending on how mad the assistant DA is."

"Sounds like a lot of police jargon to me. What does Rob do?"

"He's a deputy in the Kingsland County Sheriff's Department. And they are chronically short-staffed, which is probably why Rob is always in a bad mood. This isn't Houston or Austin, but we have our share of burglars, arsonists, drug dealers, and meth heads. The county includes Horseshoe Bay, Marble Falls, and Granite Falls, all the way out to Granite Shoals to the west and Lampasas to the north. He has a dangerous job, and we're chronically worried that he won't come home one night."

I called Mary Louise and informed her of the day's activities. It was by then four o'clock in the afternoon, and I was beginning to miss my cocktail-hour partner.

"Do you think she'll be all right?"

"I certainly hope so. That would have been a lot of work to try and do alone. I've been fortunate to have residents and fellows working with me for years, so that procedure would have been a bear solo, damn near impossible. Dick Welker helped me after he finished the forearm plating. Strong as an ox. Couldn't have done it without him. How are you? And how's the Tipster?"

"We're missing you. When will you be home?"

"I hope day after tomorrow. Julie should be stable by then. Dick is here to look after her, and her mother will make sure she's well taken care of."

"All right then. I'm starting to get ready for my donor dinner. I'll be thinking about you when I'm in the dressing process. I know how much you like to watch."

"As I've become older, to my dismay, watching is sometimes all that happens easily."

"I'm not worried. You can always try a little pill if you need it. Didn't you write yourself a prescription a while back?"

"Yes, but it's like a badge of accomplishment if you don't need it."

"I see. Well, I'm ready and waiting for you . . . anytime, badge or no badge."

I almost went to the parking lot and fired up the Tahoe, but I quickly realized after four hours of driving, the voyeur moment would be history.

"I love you, Doc Brady."

"And I love you in return, Mrs. Brady."

I was starving and needed to shower. Mary Louise had kindly made a reservation for me this morning while I was driving here, and she was able to get the same apartment on the water that we had stayed in for the past month. I checked in with the front desk, placed my parking pass on the dashboard where it would be visible to security, and parked in my assigned spot. I took a much-needed shower, opened a bottle of pinot noir compliments of the management, and stepped out onto the deck. It was a beautiful night in the Hill Country. The wine was a Texas Hill Country vintage and quite good. If I had thought about it, I would have made a side trip to the grocery and bought a few items that I could prepare in case I wanted to dine in, which I desperately did. However, having acted without much forethought, the fridge and cupboard were bare. So, I put on a pair of jeans and walked along the western edge of Lake LBJ, through the grassy expanse of the Hill Country Resort, and into the yacht club.

The yacht club was dark, lit only by table lamps and low-light chandeliers. There were bar tables adjacent to the bar, which had large-screen smart TVs, private booths for intimate conversations, and a large dining room on the other side of the bar. I ordered a

Tito's dirty martini with olives from the young waiter and perused the menu. I decided on a steak salad, which as advertised would be a salad with sliced ribeye steak mixed in, and sipped my martini, which was so cold, ice crystals were floating on top. I felt myself beginning to relax, when I felt a hand on my shoulder.

"You did some excellent work today, I hear," said Dr. Buck Owens. He was still in a coat and tie, so I assumed he must be attending a dinner meeting.

"Thanks. How did you hear about that?"

"I talked to Dick Welker. He said you were a magician in the OR."

"Well, I've had some experience with that procedure. Dick was excellent help, by the way. I couldn't have completed the procedure without him."

"That's good to hear. I always like to have outside sources confirm my opinion of our staff. Say, would you like to join us? I'm at a dinner meeting with two of our administrative folks, along with a couple of board members. I'm sure they would like to meet you."

My dinner arrived at that moment, and I opted to finish my drink, eat, and stop by his table before leaving. The steak salad was delicious. I wanted to have a second martini, but chose rather to have a glass of the house cabernet. By the time I finished, I was ready for bed, but thought it impolite to ignore Buck's offer. I wandered around toward the rear of the restaurant, finally spotting him with four other people. Everyone stood when I approached the table.

"This is the famous Dr. Jim Bob Brady," he said, as everyone stood.

"This is Lynn Abbott, director of the HR department."

I shook her hand. She was attractive, with mahogany-colored skin and braided hair, and she wore a black business suit.

"This is Bill Porter, CEO of HCMC."

We shook hands as well. Another business suit, military short haircut, and no facial hair.

"And these are two of our board members, Dr. Jackson Morse, chief of surgery, and Dr. Dan Burns, chief of anesthesiology."

We shook hands also. Both in business suits, balding, with glasses, and looked . . . well, doctorish.

Buck pulled up another chair, and we sat and kibitzed for a bit. The waitress came by and brought their food, and I ordered another cabernet. My fellow diners appeared to be drinking water. Too bad for them. We exchanged information about our backgrounds and training, and I listened to their conversations about methods to get a larger patient base and ways to cut costs and still keep up with inflationary rises in salaries and material goods needed to run the hospital. I eventually couldn't suppress a yawn, so I politely excused myself, shook everyone's hand again, and headed to my very temporary home.

The walk woke me up a bit. As I approached the condo building, I saw a flashing light ahead. Once I reached the front of the building, I saw it was an official vehicle with its roof lights flashing. The lettering on the side read Sheriff's Office, Kingsland County. I wondered if there had been a break-in or if other misdeeds had occurred on the property, but as I reached the elevator, I saw a large white man, in a khaki uniform with a holstered sidearm, standing in the lobby.

"You Brady?" he asked.

"Yes. I'm Jim Bob Brady. And you?"

"Deputy Sheriff Rob Bates."

He didn't attempt to shake my hand.

"What can I do for you, Officer?"

"You operated on my wife today. Julie Bates? Fixed her hip, or so I hear. You didn't speak to me before or after the surgery."

"I didn't see you either in the pre-op area or in the waiting room after the procedure. I spoke to Julie's mother, Lucy. If you were there, I'm sorry I missed you."

"I wasn't there because I was out chasing down criminals."

"I'm confused. How was I supposed to know to speak to you if you weren't on property before or after your wife's operation?"

"Hey, bub, don't get smart with me," he said, as he withdrew a nightstick of some sort and started rapping the palm of his hand with it.

"What's this about, Officer? I'm tired. Your wife's operation wore me out. It turned out very well. I was able to internally fixate the main portion of the pelvic fracture and replace her hip with titanium components combined with a lot of bone cement. It will take her a while to recover, but I believe she'll be fine in time. If you wanted to speak to me, you could have told Lucy, and I would have been more than happy to call you. But I didn't get that message, and I really don't appreciate your implied threat with that nightstick."

About that time, an equally large man with a hotel security badge and uniform showed up in a golf cart.

"Deputy, do we have some sort of problem here? I believe this man here is Dr. Brady, one of our guests. I've seen him several times over the past month, and I do not believe he is some sort of miscreant."

Rob Bates stared at both of us, then placed his nightstick back in its holster.

"No problem. Dr. Brady here operated on my wife today, and I was just getting the skinny on how the surgery went."

"I see. Well, it looks to me like Dr. Brady here is tired, and if you've learned what you needed to know, perhaps we can let him get some shut-eye."

That was my signal to press the elevator button. It was my good fortune to see the car was on the ground floor, so I quickly strode in, pressed the CLOSE button, and was happy to be in lift-off mode. Just prior to the door closing, a hand reached in, causing the door to open again.

"Anything going on with my wife, you talk to me, not that bitch mother of hers. Got it?"

"I'll be happy to discuss with you anything of note about your wife's condition. However, I'm ethically obligated to discuss Julie's condition with her mother as well," which was a lie, but too bad. "She's next of kin in the bloodline. You're next of kin in the relative line."

He stared at me with malevolence for a moment, then let the door close.

What was that all about?

CHAPTER 7

DEPUTY ROB BATES

In spite of the events that ended the evening, I slept like a log. The sun was beginning its morning rise when I awoke, and I jumped out of bed like I had someplace to be and was late. The clock showed 7:10. I made coffee with the house blend, whatever that was, and put on shorts, a sweatshirt, and running shoes. At the beginning of the sabbatical, Mary Louise had encouraged me to start a walking program. I was never going to be a runner. But I could walk. When you play golf, you walk more than you realize. I had a Fitbit watch, and it wasn't unusual for me to walk 8,000 steps during a round. But that was back and forth walking, and not as good for the cardiovascular system as regular walking, according to my health-conscious wife.

I finished my coffee, performed some of my morning ablutions, took the elevator to the ground floor, and started out. I walked up to the central lodge of the Hill Country Resort, felt pretty good, and kept going to the main drag through town, FM 2147. I made a U-turn and realized my mistake. I went twice as far as I should have. I limped along for a while, wondering how a guy could be so smart in surgery yet so dumb walking for exercise. After a time, a kindly worker in a four-wheeler picked me up. I sat amidst shovels and rakes, feeling pretty silly, while he drove me back to the condominium building. By then, I was really beat.

The hot shower revived me, after which I had another cup of coffee and tasted a packaged bran muffin, compliments of the resort. That was insufficient for my hunger, so I drove into Marble Falls and had breakfast at the Blue Bonnet Cafe. It was open for breakfast and lunch only. I feasted on country fried steak, fried eggs over easy, and hash browns. I couldn't tell Mary Louise, which was about the only sort of secret I ever kept from her. I remembered a lunch I had in Houston with some of my colleagues during a Saturday downpour that rained-out golf. I came home and told her I ate a salad with a little protein. In reality, we had gone to an In-N-Out Burger, and I had eaten a Double-Double with all the trimmings. At the time, I reasoned that lettuce, tomato, onions, jalapeños, and pickles comprised a salad . . . and as for the protein, well, there were the two hamburger patties.

From the Blue Bonnet I went back out to Granite Falls to the Hill Country Medical Center. Business must have been good, as the parking lot was full. I pulled into a DOCTORS ONLY parking spot and hoped for the best. I called Mary Louise from the car.

"Morning, love. Did you sleep all right without me?"

"No," I lied. "Tossed and turned. You?"

"Life is never as good without you. Did you get something to eat?"

"Yes I did. I'm at the hospital, going in to see how Julie Bates is doing."

"I'd asked you where you had breakfast, but I know you won't tell me you went to the Blue Bonnet and had a chicken fried steak."

"Guilty. It probably knocked maybe five minutes off my life span. Sorry."

"It's a rare treat. I'll chalk it up to the fact you were missing me, and food helped ease the pain."

"My thoughts exactly. I'll call you later."

I rode up to the third floor, temporary home of the hospital inpatients. I wandered down to the nursing station and inquired as to the location of Julie Bates's room. The ward clerk looked up at me, stood and looked at my Tommy Bahama shirt, blue jeans, and ostrich boots, and asked me if I was a relative.

"No, ma'am, I'm her surgeon. Dr. Jim Bob Brady," I said, and extended a hand in greeting.

She returned the handshake and said, "Well, don't that beat all," and directed me to Julie's room.

Lucy was sitting in a bedside chair. She stood and gave me a hug.

"How's she doing?"

"She had a decent night. Slept on and off. She has a morphine pump, and she had to press the button a few extra times, but all in all, pretty good. She's been awake and talking, so that's a good sign."

"Great." I pulled back the covers and checked her dressing and the sump drain I placed during surgery to remove blood that would accumulate after the procedure. The receptacle had a small amount of blood in it, a good sign. The outside portion of the dressing was intact and dry, also a good sign.

"Not much blood. That's remarkable for that much dissection. She's a good clotter."

Lucy laughed. "A good clotter. Sounds like an epitaph to me," and laughed again, covering her mouth as to avoid waking her daughter.

"I had a visitor last night: Deputy Sheriff Rob Bates. He seemed to be upset that I hadn't spoken to him after the surgery." I related the events to Lucy.

"Oh, my, I'm so sorry. He can be such an ass. I'm glad the security guard came along when he did."

"You certainly don't think he would have done me bodily harm, do you? The surgeon who had earlier that day fixed his wife's hip?"

"You never know with that man," she said, looking aside.

"Lucy, when I met you, and you had the black eye. That wasn't from a cabinet, was it?"

She hesitated, then teared up, and shook her head.

"It was your son-in-law?"

She nodded.

"What prompted that sort of behavior, to slug his mother-in-law?"

Lucy composed herself. "He and Julie have been separated, and she was living with me. My husband died a few years ago, and it's so lonely at home . . . so I was happy to have her there. She works here, you know, as a radiology technician, so it was convenient. We worked the same shift and could share a ride to and from work. She'd been having trouble with Rob for a while. His violent episodes, and wild tirades, and coming home drunk. He'd slapped her around a few times, hitting her in areas that don't show with clothes on, like her abdomen and kidney areas. She had tried to get pregnant for a very long time, then last year it finally happened for her. But Rob came home meaner than a snake one night, knocked her around, and within two days she miscarried. That's when she left and moved in with me.

"So a couple of weeks ago, he comes by the house after work, drunk, and starts banging on the front door. Julie didn't want to see him, so I went to the door. I opened it but left the screen door closed. He tried to open it and finally broke the lock as I was trying to secure it. It slipped out of my hand, he pulled, then slammed it against my face. Thus the black eye. Julie heard the ruckus, came running, and finally got him settled down and out of there."

"You told me they were coming out of a movie together when she was run over. How did that come about?"

"They had been having date night once a week, trying to get back together. She still loves him, you know, in spite of it all. She blames it on his work and the kind of people he has to deal with on a daily basis. It's like he's taking on the personality of the people he's putting in jail. Julie thinks if he had a job change, he would be normal again. But Rob loves being a cop and really hasn't had enough education to do anything else, except low-paying menial jobs. And trust me, he's not going to change careers anytime soon. He loves the power."

"Sorry you have to deal with that. What about law enforcement?"

"Law enforcement? He IS law enforcement. I called the Granite Falls Police Department during one of his tirades one night in the front yard. And while they did show up, it turns out that both officers who came to my house knew Rob, even though he's with the sheriff's department. There is a lot of overlap between the police department, who handles city issues, and sheriff's, who handles county issues. As far as I'm concerned, they are all in the same boat together. The two police officers managed to calm Rob down and sent him home. They asked me if I wanted to press charges, but they allowed as how what were they supposed to charge him with? Yelling at his estranged wife in his mother-in-law's front yard? They both laughed at that. I sent them on their way. They won't do anything unless Rob kills one of us, and even then, I'm not so sure how that would pan out. Law enforcement officers stick together, as far as I'm concerned. Protect and Serve applies more to the officers themselves rather than the citizens."

"Lucy, I find that hard to believe. I'm well acquainted with the hierarchy of the Houston Police Department. The former chief of police and his daughter, the current chief of police, have been good friends of mine for a long time. Protect and Serve is their motto. They are model officers in the law enforcement system, and they strive to impart that philosophy to all their employees."

"Doc Brady, this isn't Houston. This is Granite Falls in Kingsland County, where the good ol' boys stick together. Don't forget about Rob showing up at your hotel and brandishing his nightstick at you. That was real police work around here, finding someone's location in order to intimidate them. How'd he even know where you were staying? Did you think about that? You'd better watch your step, son."

CHAPTER 8

THE DRIVE

I wasn't quite ready for lunch due to the late breakfast at the Blue Bonnet Cafe, so I decided to take a drive. I entered Highway 71, went east for a bit, then turned north onto Highway 281. I passed through the town of Marble Falls, then drove up to Burnet. There were so many retail establishments, you could hardly tell when one town stopped and the other began. There were numerous auto dealerships, a John Deere dealership, fast-food eateries, barbecue haunts, bars, gas stations, car washes, an H-E-B plus! and a Walmart Supercenter.

I made a U-turn in Burnet and headed south to FM 1431, then headed east toward Granite Shoals and Kingsland. I found a public viewing area on Lake LBJ, parked, and viewed the lake from the north side. We had stayed on the south side of the lake, so I wanted to see if the scenery was any different. It wasn't. The Ferguson power plant was visible from both the north and south viewpoints, seeing how it sat on Lake LBJ and was a massive structure, providing power to a large portion of the area. The water looked the same, as did the distant buildings.

I got back in the car, now hungry from my excursion, and found the Crazy Gals Cafe. I entered and sat down, ordered a Coke, and perused the menu. I chose what the locals would probably call the "heartstopper": a bacon and fried-egg cheeseburger. While I waited, I noticed a newspaper stand nearby and retrieved the local paper, the *Highlander*. According to the legend below the title, this paper served Marble Falls, Granite Falls, Kingsland and Burnet Counties, and the Highland Lakes area. The top half of the front page lauded the local high school football team for winning their tenth straight game. The Mustangs were headed to the state championship.

The bottom half of the page contained an article about missing women from the area. Over the past twelve months, six women had disappeared. Two were from Marble Falls, one from Granite Falls, one from Granite Shoals, one from Highland Haven, and one from Horseshoe Bay. All six disappearances had been investigated by law enforcement, including the police department from each of the cities plus sheriff's deputies from Kingsland, Burnet and Llano counties. So far, there were no clues as to the fate or whereabouts of the missing women. No evidence of foul play, no post-disappearance use of credit cards or ATMs. It's like they were here one minute, gone the next.

My lunch was served, and I must say, if there was a better cheeseburger, I had never eaten it. I had to ask for extra napkins due to the juice from the fried egg and the medium-rare patty, which was advertised to be premium ground chuck beef. My oh my, was it good. Once I finished, I stopped by the kitchen, said thanks to the cook, overtipped the waitress and, because I felt a nap coming on, decided to go straight back to the hotel.

I headed west on FM 1431, turned south on a couple of paved county roads, and connected back with Highway 71. I was almost to the FM 2147 turnoff to Granite Falls when I noticed a siren and a blinking light behind me. Thinking it was an ambulance, or a law enforcement vehicle after a miscreant—or maybe someone had discovered the fate of the missing women—I pulled onto FM 2147 and stopped on the gravel shoulder, right next to where the Horseshoe Bay police officer hides to give unsuspecting tourists tickets for traveling over the posted speed limit of 45 mph. He honked at me and waved through his open driver door to move on, when suddenly the emergency vehicle pulled in right behind me.

Deputy Sheriff Rob Bates got out of his car, sidled up to my window, and put his hands on the door frame. "I thought I told you to talk to *me* about my wife, not her mother."

"Yes, you did, and I allowed as how I wasn't going to do that. This is worth a traffic stop?"

"Get out of the vehicle, Brady."

I stayed put.

"I said, get out—"

"What the hell is going on?" asked the Horseshoe Bay police officer who had now exited his vehicle and was walking toward us, and not in a good mood. "You're interfering with official police business."

"You mean this pissant of a speed trap?" said Bates. "My business takes precedence over yours. I'm Deputy Rob Bates, Kingsland County, and this man is about to be under arrest."

"What the hell for?" I asked.

"You keep your mouth shut," Bates said.

"Now wait a minute, Bates," said the police officer. "First of all, what's he done? Secondly, you're in my jurisdiction. This is Horseshoe Bay city limits, and you have no authority here."

Bates pulled up his trousers and his gun belt, like in the movies. This was interesting, except for the part about my going to jail.

"What's he done, Bates?" the police officer asked again, when he arrived at my car.

"Nothing," I said. "I was just taking a drive around the lake, had lunch at the Crazy Gals Cafe, and am on the way back to the Hill Country Resort. I'm staying there temporarily. I'm an orthopedic surgeon from Houston, and I was called in to do a complicated hip surgery on this man's wife yesterday."

The HSB officer looked at me, then at Bates.

"Is that right? So what's he done, Bates?"

Bates was silent. Just stared at the other officer and nodded.

"I know about you, Bates. You're a cowboy with a bad temper. I can't imagine what you could be after the doctor for. Sounds like he did you a big favor, coming here from Houston to operate on your wife. I don't know what he did to piss you off, but knowing your history, it was something valid only in that twisted mind of yours."

"Now you wait just a—"

"Doctor, continue on with your journey. And I'm sorry we have the likes of this man in local law enforcement. Please accept my apology. You can be on your way. I'll deal with Bates here."

With that, he tipped his hat at me, and I took that as my signal to head home. The bed in my apartment wasn't like home, but it was a lot better than jail.

"What in the world is going on over there?" asked Mary Louise, after my recitation of the afternoon events. "Why does this guy have a vendetta against you? You've done nothing to him except bail his wife out of a terrible situation."

"I think I mentioned to you that Lucy, her mother, told me that her daughter told her that she thought her husband had pushed her into the path of the car that caused the damage. I haven't asked her about that issue again, but if Bates did that, or thinks the wife might have told us something to that effect, he would be in serious trouble. I think he's posturing himself to be as intimidating as possible to me, thinking he can scare me off. He doesn't know me very well, does he?"

"Dog with a bone, that's you. Once you get something going in your head, look out."

"By the way, there was an article in the *Highlander,* the local paper, about some missing women. Had you heard anything about that during the month we were here?"

"Maybe, but I think we were both caught up in your sabbatical, and I was worried about how you would feel about not getting up and going to work for the first time in thirty years. I'm not sure we even looked at a newspaper during that month. And I don't remember hearing it on the news, so it hasn't made national headlines yet."

"I brought the newspaper back to the apartment with me. I'll finish reading the article and see what I can find out online."

"Are you coming home tomorrow?"

"I plan to. I'll make rounds in the morning—I guess with one patient, that would be 'round'—and if Julie is doing well, I'll probably leave. I can pull her drain and Hemovac and check the wound. After forty-eight hours, she'll be able to get up into a chair. Originally I thought she'd have to be in bed for six weeks due to the pelvic fracture, but since I was able to internally fixate the large piece, she can probably at least sit in a chair. I want to try and help Lucy get her approved to go the rehab unit at HCMC. She'll need at least three weeks before she can be ambulatory, and therefore she needs to be in a post-op care facility. Her mother could not handle her at home, much less attend to her duties here at the hospital AND take care of her daughter."

"Did you get something to eat?"

"I did, but late. I'm totally off schedule here. I'm worn out, and think I'll turn on some mindless television and nod off. Sweet dreams."

"You too, sweetie. See you tomorrow."

I was thrilled she didn't ask me what I had for lunch.

CHAPTER 9

DISAPPEARING WOMEN

When you fall asleep at eight in the evening, there is a good chance you'll awaken at four thirty in the morning, those magic eight hours having been completed. I tossed and turned for a bit, then resigned myself to the fact I might as well get up. I brewed the hotel packet coffee, then sat on the deck. It was still dark, but the property was lit well by a number of round bulbs strung over restaurant patios and the beach bar and between palm trees. The Ferguson power plant was also a source of light that reflected across Lake LBJ. The lighting gave the property a Christmas feel to it, warm and inviting.

When the sun began to rise, an orange glow was cast over the water, which, combined with the string lights still bright, gave me a feeling of joy and happiness. Probably that's how an early caveman felt when, in his sojourns for food, he stumbled across a more advanced tribe than his, who had already discovered fire. Fire provided light, warmth, the opportunity to eat cooked food and, maybe in some circumstances, additional weaponry. I couldn't imagine a world without light and fire. I pondered the lifespan of our ancestors from that era and figured it must have been exceptionally short.

I stepped inside for more coffee and a blanket, when I spied the *Highlander* newspaper from the Crazy Gals Cafe. I thumbed through it while the coffee brewed. Most of the story was on the front page, but there were a few more details near the back of the paper. The paper's synopsis concluded the women were of similar age, ranging from thirty-seven to fifty-two. Four of the women had children, but none of the children were living at home. All the victims worked, including two nurses from HCMC. All the women were married, including one to a husband who was in law enforcement. There were no clues of any kind. The presumption was a serial kidnapper/rapist/murderer was on the loose. Women had been told to avoid being alone, be fearful of strangers, and carry Mace or bear spray to ward off potential attacks. The paper discouraged women from carrying firearms, unless they had a concealed weapon permit. My take on that? This is Texas, and I would bet good money most women were packing, regardless of a permit status.

That was all that was available, so I went online, typed in *kidnapping, disappearances,* and *Hill Country,* and got a number of hits. There was one article that named all the women and described their lives in detail. It was written by a graduate student in journalism at the University of Texas in Austin. I was handicapped somewhat by not having a printer, so I got dressed, went to the ground floor, and walked over to the resort's business center. Entrance was granted by swiping the room-card key. I found a printer that I was familiar with, married the USB cable to my smart phone, and pressed PRINT. I had to reload the paper tray once but finally got all the data, which was about twenty-five pages' worth.

I went back to the apartment, made more coffee, and started to read.

Margaret Harris, age 37, last seen November of last year. She worked as a dispatcher for the Big Tex Trucking Company in Marble Falls. Her husband was a detective in the Granite Falls Police Department. No children. She left work around six o'clock in the evening and wasn't seen again. He was on duty, investigating a shooting in Granite Falls, and through GPS tracking records of the city vehicle he was driving, he was never in position to be involved in the kidnapping.

Katie Smith, age 52, last seen January of this year. She worked in the hospitality business at Hill Country Resort. Her husband was a dentist who had offices in Granite Falls and Marble Falls. She had two grown children, one in Austin and the other in Dallas. She left work around eight thirty in the evening, after a function she was in charge of, and never came home. Her husband's alibi was that he was home packing for a dental convention in Dallas the next day. There was no confirmation of this.

Carla Robinson, age 44, disappeared March 9. She worked as a nurse on the three-to-eleven evening shift at Hill Country Medical Center. Her husband was a long-haul trucker and worked for Big Tex Trucking Company, same firm as Margaret Harris. She had one child, who was in her last year of college at Texas State in San Marcos. She left work about eleven thirty, with no sign of her since. Her husband was delivering a load in Biloxi, Mississippi, confirmed by the company, and couldn't have been in two places at the same time.

Karen Statton, age 48, vanished May 13. She was an ICU nurse at HCMC on the day shift, seven in the morning to three in the afternoon. She didn't show up for her five o'clock weekly canasta game with friends. Her husband worked as an engineer at the Ferguson power plant. They had one son, in medical school in Houston. Mr. Statton was at bowling night on a team sponsored by his employer. Records at Ferguson's HR department confirmed the team was at the bowling alley from six to ten in the evening. He had gone directly there from work.

Jorja Watson, age 39, disappeared on July 11. She was a real estate broker and, with her husband, owned Bay Country Realty. She disappeared during the day, around eleven in the morning, after showing a lakefront property to an out-of-town couple. She didn't show up for her next scheduled appointment. They had no children. The husband was running an open house from one to six in the afternoon, and video records from the street cameras showed his car never left the house.

Last was Hilary Allen, age 46, who went missing September 17. She was vice president of a local bank, Lake Savings and Trust. She didn't return to work after a business lunch at Forno's, a lakefront casual restaurant. She and her husband had three children: one in law school, one a senior in college, and one out of school and working. Her husband was a litigation lawyer in Austin, and he was at the office preparing for a trial that began the next day. He stayed in an apartment in Austin during the week and came home on weekends. His staff documented his whereabouts the day of his wife's disappearance.

Six missing women, six husbands, and not a clue in any of the cases. Except for the dentist at home and packing with no alibi, all the husbands had documentation of their respective whereabouts. The gist I got from reading the files was that the husbands weren't suspects. The detectives involved were looking elsewhere for a perpetrator, some sort of serial killer. Granite Falls PD had called in an FBI profiler, whose main conclusion after reviewing all the information was that in keeping with the past pattern of a woman disappearing every two months, there should be another event this month, November. And all law enforcement personnel should be on the lookout, but for exactly what, I couldn't decipher.

CHAPTER 10

JULIE BATES

"There you are. I was getting a little worried about you," said Mary Louise when I called.

"I'm fine, just got sidetracked reading about those missing women. That *Highlander* article was pretty superficial, so I googled the subject and found a few articles, the best of which was by a grad student in journalism at UT. She listed the women by name, discussed their jobs, their husbands' jobs, their children, when they went missing. I'm intrigued by the whole thing. No clues, no signs of foul play, no credit card or ATM usage by the victims. I hesitate to use the word 'victim,' because there is no evidence that any of the women have been kidnapped or are deceased. Of course, there is no evidence that any of them are at liberty or alive, either."

"It does sound . . . interesting, but depressing at the same time. What were you thinking you could do about it?"

"Well," I laughed weakly, "find them, I guess. But seriously, I have no power any longer. When I've 'looked into things' in the past, I had originally Chief Stan Lombardo to back me up, then Chief Susan Beeson, his daughter, to keep me out of trouble. Now, I have no means to investigate anything that might be either of interest or that might provide insight into a murky situation."

"Well, you do have J. J., and he's certainly been helpful in the past."

Our son, J. J., owned a private investigation firm called B&B Investigations, a company he and his best friend and former college roommate Brad Broussard started during their senior year of college at the University of Texas. They had done work for all sorts of entities, such as governmental agencies, the Houston Police Department, charitable organizations with suspected malfeasance, and individuals with wives or husbands with "wandering eyes," as he described it. He had helped me out in the past with my meddling into other people's affairs, starting years ago when our neighbor's child had been run over and killed in the street. He and Brad were excellent at obtaining information and decoding the root of past calamities which other investigative firms had been unable to decipher.

"I guess I could give him a call, see if he and Brad might shed more light on the situation."

"That sounds grand. Are you coming home today?"

"That's my plan, provided Deputy Bates doesn't put me in jail and throw away the key for perceived crimes. I have a mind to go see the sheriff of Kingsland County and get this jerk off my back."

"Settle down, boy. Pack up your belongings, go see your patient, and get out of there and come home to me and your faithful canine."

I showered and shaved, packed the meager items I'd bought along on the trip, and headed over to HCMC. I found a parking spot for visitors, entered the lobby, and spotted Lucy Williams sitting at the receptionist's desk.

"Good morning," she said, standing to greet me.

"How's our patient?"

"Alert. Maybe you can introduce yourself. She's never met you—she's been either unconscious or sleeping each time you've seen her."

"Of course, you're right. Want to come with me? I have to pull her drain and disconnect the Hemovac, then change her dressing."

"Yes, I'll get one of the volunteers to take over for me."

As we walked, I said, "Not one to complain about your son-in-law, but he somehow followed me yesterday after I left here. It's almost like he has a tracking device on my car. I took a drive around the lake, had lunch in Granite Shoals, and was on my way back when he pulled me over at the entrance to FM 2147. Luckily there was a Horseshoe Bay traffic cop sitting in that speed trap on the south side of the intersection who came to my rescue."

"I apologize. The guy is a nut job."

"Hard to argue with that, Lucy."

Julie was sitting up in bed when we walked in. Her hair was combed, and I noticed a little makeup and lipstick had been applied. I introduced myself.

"I'd shake your hand, Dr. Brady, but I have a cast on my right arm and an IV line in my left. Thanks for fixing me up."

"You're most welcome. Your mother here is quite the persistent advocate. She convinced me to return here from Houston three days after I left. Your surgery went well, although the injury was a complicated one, but ultimately you'll be fine. How's your pain level?"

"On a scale of one to ten, it's been a twelve. The pain is better today, but I don't want to let go of my little friend, here," she said, indicating the morphine pump button that was attached to her IV line.

I went into some detail about repairing the pelvic fracture and the difficulty in performing the hip replacement and why the area was lathered in quite a bit of bone cement.

"Will I set off the security alarm at the airport?"

"Absolutely. We'll get you a laminated card that apprises Homeland Security of your hardware. I'd like to change the dressing now."

I put on sterile gloves. The layered bandage was pristine clean, and the incision was soft, not red, no signs of infection. I pulled the drain, disconnected the Hemovac, and redressed the wound with the help of head nurse Louann Simms, whom I had met in the ER on the day of surgery.

"Looks mighty good, Doc," said Louann. "Clean as a veritable whistle. I'm glad you were able to return and get this mess fixed up."

"Thanks much. Looks like I'll be heading back to Houston shortly, ladies. Lucy, thanks for calling me. I was glad to be of service. Julie, it's been a pleasure. Dr. Welker will take over your care in my absence. He did a nice job repairing the forearm fracture. He'll be consulting with me, and if there are any unusual problems, 'I shall return,' to quote General Douglas MacArthur."

Lucy game me a hug, and her daughter said goodbye with a finger wave on the cast side, and I left the hospital sector of the medical center.

On my way out, I ran into Dr. Buck Owens. "It's been a real pleasure to meet you, Jim. Many thanks for coming to the rescue. We would be thrilled to have you on our staff, if just to take on these complex cases that we would otherwise have to refer to Austin. As you can see, we have the facilities to handle any kind of injury or medical problem; we just don't have the staff yet."

"I'll take that offer under advisement, Buck. I appreciate your hospitality, as well as your willingness to forgo all the formalities and allow me operating privileges at the hospital without all the red tape. That was above and beyond the call of duty but certainly sped up the process of getting Julie Bates's hip repaired."

"Safe travels," he said, and shook my hand.

CHAPTER 11

"THE TIMES, THEY ARE A-CHANGIN'"
(BOB DYLAN, 1964)

I sped out of town, turned onto Highway 71 and sped toward Austin, keeping an eye on my rear view and side mirrors for Deputy Bates. Fortunately, I was out of his county shortly after departure, so I had an uneventful drive home.

Tip acted as though I had been gone for years, jumping around like a silly puppy might have done. He was so exuberant I was worried he might sprain a joint. Mary Louise, on the other hand, was coy, and dressed in a sheer negligee that would be a fitting addition to a Victoria's Secret catalog. We kissed and pressed our bodies together. I felt little Jim Bob Brady take over from big Jim Bob Brady, and I lost all thought of anything except making love to this fabulous woman. I patted Tip on the head and told him I'd see him in a while.

We were starving after our post-reunion nap, and since it was near the cocktail hour, we poured ourselves a glass of Ridge chardonnay into a roadie cup and took Tip downstairs for a walk. We let him run in the dog park, sniffing and smelling and cavorting and having a grand old time with his fellow canines. Mary Louise had prepared for us to eat in, so after Tip's walk, we dined on Caesar salad, cold boiled shrimp, and crab legs, with just enough horse-radish in the red sauce to make one's eyes water after devouring a bite. We finished the wine, opened another bottle, this time a Rombauer chardonnay, and finished most of that watching a couple of episodes of *Breaking Bad*.

All in all, it was a splendid day.

The next week or two passed slowly for me. I felt restless. I played golf a few times, only during the week, since our club was down in Sugarland, twenty or thirty minutes away, and weekend traffic was abysmal. I would have much preferred to belong to one of the old staid country clubs in the downtown/medical center/Rice University area, but those clubs were primarily for legacy boys, not an army colonel's son from Waco.

Mary Louise had her charity boards and still enjoyed participating in fundraisers, and she seemed content to continue with her activities as usual. She really enjoyed having me home during this sabbatical; why, I don't know. Sometimes I couldn't stand myself, so how could she? To keep busy, I read novels and newspapers, watched the news, walked for exercise, and in general kept myself active enough to stay out of trouble, especially by avoiding drinking during the day. Moving the cocktail hour from 5 p.m. to say, noon, would be the kiss of death for a retiree.

But I was bored. How could I not be, after all those years of working fifty to sixty hours a week? I used to complain about the work, but I found myself missing it. Not so much the paperwork, or the insurance calls justifying my intended operations, or the potential malpractice lawsuits in Houston and the surrounding area, one of the plaintiff lawyers' favorite cities in which to file. I missed the patient contact, the interaction with my colleagues, the challenge of a difficult case such as the one I had recently performed in Granite Falls. I felt like I wanted to work, needed to work, even, but on my own terms, without the excess baggage of insurance bureaucracy I had been working under these past many years.

I began to think of life in Granite Falls, able to work the hours that made me happy, see the patients I wanted to see, operate on those patients I wanted to help. It would be a totally different experience with a new approach to medicine, and perhaps, as Dr. Buck Owens suggested, I would find other outlets to help folks other than direct patient care, in addition to the selective practice I could design for myself.

Mary Louise and I were unencumbered. Our only child, J. J., was in his mid-30s and had found a lovely girl to marry. Her name was Kathryn Hicks, a graduate of the SMU business school, and the product of a well-connected family from Dallas. Her father owned several banks in the Dallas-Ft. Worth Metroplex. He was an avid golfer and liked his single-malt scotch, so we had interests in common. Kathryn had followed her father into the banking business. J. J. and Brad had opened an office in Dallas, and J. J. spent most of his time working there, while Brad came to be in charge of the Houston office.

J. J. and Kathryn had a destination wedding at the Hill Country Resort, a property we'd come to know quite well over the past few years. We loved the Lake LBJ water view, and while not unlike our former view in Galveston, it did not come with the threat of seasonal hurricanes.

We had sold our Galveston house on the ocean side of the island once we became regular visitors to Hill Country. We had endured one hurricane, four tropical storms, and three storm surges, courtesy of the ocean. The landscaping and decking out to the beach had washed away twice, not to mention the angst of worrying about the property from June to October each and every year.

It became too much. We sold the property to a younger couple, and at their insistence, had included all the furniture, the audio-visual equipment, the dishes and cookware, and even the red, white, and blue robes Mary Louise had purchased for the guest rooms. The buyers were from Houston and were well aware of the vagaries of the hurricane season in the Gulf of Mexico, so our conscience was clear after the sale.

Mary Louise and I were having lunch at Jason's Deli, and I decided it was a good time to ask what she thought about possibly moving to the Granite Falls area.

"I knew that was coming," she said. "I can tell you're getting bored, even though you're only in the second month of your sabbatical. You're thinking that you would like to continue to work, but not at the pace you have been working these past thirty years. And with the clinic situation at University Orthopedic, you have to work full time to maintain your overhead costs. Whereas at Hill County Medical Center, you're an employee of the hospital and can adjust your work schedule more to your individual needs rather than the financial requirements necessary to run a large practice. With that in mind, I have something to show you," she said, and opened her purse—which was large enough to be an overnight bag—and pulled out a sheaf of papers.

"What's this?"

"Houses for sale with a lake view."

If I was a sentimental, sappy old fool, I might have shed a tear. As it was, being the manly man, I reached over and hugged her, but couldn't speak for a moment.

"How did you . . . ?"

"We've been married thirty-five years, Jim Bob Brady, and I know you better than you know yourself. I've said to you more times than I can remember that there are two things in life that are most important to me. One, I want you to be happy. Two, I go where you go. Look through the paperwork, check the houses that you want to see, and I'll call the realtor. I've called the resort and booked that top-floor condo for tomorrow, with an open-ended departure."

That was a speechless lunch for me.

CHAPTER 12

J. J.

I had kept in touch with Lucy Williams, checking on her daughter's progress while I was home in Houston. Due to the severity of her injuries, and procedural but creative coding on the insurance company billing documents, Julie Bates had been allowed to remain in the hospital until the wound had healed and the sutures were removed. Subsequently, she was admitted to HCMC's rehabilitation unit and was approved for thirty days. This was a godsend for both Lucy and Julie, who could remain under direct nursing and physical therapy supervision until she was ambulatory. These positive occurrences in her care came about through the influence of Dr. Dick Welker, aided and abetted by Dr. Buck Owens. I believed the staff I had come in contact with at HCMC were primarily about providing excellent care to the patient and did not allow a few stumbling blocks to limit them in achieving that goal.

We decided to caravan over to Granite Falls, me in my Chevy Tahoe with Tip, Mary Louise in her cute red Porsche SUV. I called the color "arrest-me red," but the few times she had been stopped for driving above the indicated speed limit, she had driven away unscathed and without a ticket. It must be nice to exude such charm and panache.

I called Dr. Buck Owens's office on the drive over to tell them we were returning and were planning to look at some houses. His administrative assistant, which was Lucy Williams's official title, told me he was in a meeting but would return my call soon. She was thrilled, and she asked if I would stop by and visit Julie in rehab upon my return. Most certainly I would, I told her.

I also called J. J., who happened to be in his office in Dallas.

"Morning, Pop," he said.

"Morning, son. How's it going up in the Big D?"

"Very well. We're almost as busy here as we are in Houston, and this office has only been open for three years. I'm very pleased, but Kathryn gets tired of the travel I'm required to do to see and communicate with clients. Emailing, texting, and Skype only go so far in this business. People want to see my smiling face. So I've been looking at private jets. Brad is doing a lot of business travel as well, and we've looked at the numbers of commercial travel versus private travel. What's your take on the subject?"

"In my experience, commercial is far and away the cheapest. You can join a jet service like Citation and have a contract for a certain number of hours of flying. When the hours expire, you re-enlist, if you will. Owning a jet, however, is a whole different level of cost. When I was involved in a limited partnership a few years back, we signed up for a program where my partners and I purchased the jet on credit and leased it out. The owners were allowed to use it on a limited basis and still had to pay for private travel, but only for the cost of fuel and pilot time, though for the size of the plane, two pilots were necessary. Unfortunately, we didn't get the amount of leasing income we anticipated, and with all the maintenance and equipment upgrades required by the manufacturer and the FAA, and the debt service, it turned out to be a bust.

"But your mom and I sure loved the ease of private travel. No lines in the airport, no Homeland Security patting us down, no delays or canceled flights. I couldn't deduct the costs, because I wasn't traveling to see patients and perform surgery. In your business, you'd be using the aircraft to see clients, so that would be a deductible item. You would have to run the numbers and see. Of course, you can't put a price tag on convenience or on the safety of having two pilots and limited passengers, so you'll have to enter that factor into the equation. Honestly, though, my overall opinion is don't buy an airplane unless you have unlimited funds."

He laughed. "Always a bottom-line sort of guy, aren't you, Pop?"

"Yep. But I'm happy that you're doing well enough to even be considering buying an airplane. Listen, the reason I called."

"I was certain there was a catch here."

"No catch, just need some information, and you're the best man I know for acquiring information that is not supposed to be uncovered."

I told him about the missing women in the Highland Lakes area, and that I wondered if by any chance there was a common thread among them, something that tied them all together.

"Pop, isn't this a police matter?"

"Yes. I've read the updates in the *Highlander*, the local paper, and reviewed a lengthy article by a journalism grad student at UT who dug deeper into the women's private lives. She wrote that an FBI profiler had been consulted, without any results other than there should be another kidnapping in November; the article was written before then. As far as I can tell, there was none, at least in the area where the other women disappeared. I don't know if the search for a missing woman in November was expanded outside the area, or if it was confined to the locale where the other six had disappeared. I'd appreciate you taking a look at it. Bill me for your time. I can afford it now, as long as I don't buy an airplane."

We arrived at Hill Country Resort, checked in, and were escorted to our top-floor suite by an enterprising young man. He offered a tour of the property at an hourly rate, plus transportation services to and from local restaurants as well as Austin.

"Just so you know, sir," he said, "the local police departments—Granite Falls, Marble Falls, Horseshoe Bay—keep a close lookout for visitors driving around the city after drinking, so I strongly suggest you consider hiring a driver to take you from place to place."

"Thanks, young man, but we've been here a number of times and know our way around, and we know better than to drink and drive. But we might use your services to go to Austin. Give me your card."

He did so, and I of course overtipped him and sent him on his way.

"We might use him if we want to go to dinner and a concert in Austin. He should be fairly trustworthy, since he's employed by the resort. I forgot to ask him what kind of car he had."

"Don't forget Lyft and Uber. They're usually the most cost effective," said Mary Louise.

"Uber has had some negative PR lately. I want to make sure we're safe if we're traveling in someone else's vehicle. A private driver seems the optimal method."

Once he'd left, Mary Louise asked, "What are you going to do now, husband of mine?"

"Well, I thought I would take Tip for a walk, then go over to the hospital and see Julie Bates, maybe check in with Buck Owens."

"I'm hungry. Why don't we go to the Lantana Grill and get some lunch. You can make a trip to the hospital after, while I get with the real estate agent and schedule some home tours. Sound good?"

"Absolutely." I took Tip downstairs for a stroll while Mary Louise unpacked. There were all sorts of new smells for Tip, apparently, since he lingered over every bush and blade of grass. We were steps away from the lake, and when he walked closest to the water, his ears perked up as he stared into the depths. Fish!

After a superb lunch, I headed to HCMC and parked in another DOCTORS ONLY spot. When I walked into the lobby and headed toward Lucy Williams's desk, I noticed several women gathered around her. She was crying.

"Lucy, what's wrong?" I asked.

"It's Julie. Her hip is killing her. She told me her husband came to see her early this morning, before daylight. They got into an argument, and he ended up pounding her recently operated hip and thigh with his fist, according to her. There is a very light staff on the eleven to seven night shift since it's a rehab unit and not an acute-care ward. She started screaming after he struck her, but when the nurse arrived at her room, Julie was alone. Presumably Rob left quickly, so none of the staff saw him. Julie's in X-ray now."

Radiology was on the entry floor, so I walked quickly over to review the films. A radiologist was in the reading room, going over the films.

"Jim Brady," I said, shaking his hand. "What do you think?"

"Paul Griffin," he said. "The hip and pelvis look unchanged from the postoperative films taken three weeks ago. I don't see any displacement of the prostheses, and the pelvic fracture looks to be healing fine. I would call it soft-tissue trauma at this point."

"I agree. Thanks, Paul."

"I hear you may be coming on board, Jim. We would be honored to have you. That is a pretty spectacular piece of surgery you did on that hip. I saw the pre-operative films. Nice going."

"Thanks again. Is Julie still here?"

"She should be."

I left the viewing room and walked out to the holding area. Julie was on a stretcher, accompanied by a young woman I didn't recognize.

"Hey, Julie, how are you feeling?"

"Pretty bad, Dr. Brady. Thanks so much for coming. Did you see the films?"

"Yes. They look fine. May I examine your hip?"

"Of course."

I pulled the hospital gown up, exposing her lower abdomen, hip, and pelvis. The entire area was red, and the tissue felt doughy. It would be too early for bruising. That would take a day or two to show up. Her wound was healed, without signs of disruption. I put her hip through a gentle range of motion, which did not cause her any discomfort out of the ordinary.

"Julie, the X-rays look fine, the motion in the hip seems normal, and your wound has not come undone. There is redness, and probably will be bruising tomorrow, but the trauma doesn't appear to have caused any long-term damage."

"Thanks so much," she said, holding my hand. "This is my friend Greta."

I shook Greta's hand. She was in her late thirties or early forties and had brown hair and dark eyebrows and lashes, not unattractive, but no raving beauty. She was very shy and turned away from my gaze.

"Do you work here?" I asked.

"Yes, sir, in the rehab unit. I was there when Rob beat on her hip. I didn't see him, but I heard her screaming and ran as fast as I could to her bedside. He was already gone when I got there."

"Why don't we lay off the rehab for today, let Julie rest. Tomorrow we'll resume, if she's better."

"I'll go up and let the day shift know. Nice to meet you, Dr. Brady."

Once she left, I asked Julie if she was going to file charges against her husband for assault, but that produced loud wailing and such a flow of tears that I patted her hand and walked away.

CHAPTER 13

LAW ENFORCEMENT

Being a suspicious sort, the thought crossed my mind that perhaps Julie's injury was self-inflicted. I would hate to learn that was the case, after all that work in surgery to repair the hip and pelvis. And I did like her mother, and learning her daughter injured herself would be devastating to her. The magic disappearance of Rob, the alleged offender, bothered me. I understood the staffing problem in rehab, but with only twelve beds, one would think he would be easily seen unless Greta was off the floor or otherwise indisposed. I didn't want to think the worst of my patient, so I tabled the discussion with myself.

I called Mary Louise and gave her a brief summary of Julie Bates's plight.

"Jim Bob Brady, you stay away from her husband. He has it in for you already, and confronting him could push him over the edge. I don't want you injured, or worse."

"Got it. I promise I will leave it alone for now. So, what's our plan?"

"The agent has a couple of places we can see today. Neither is occupied. Meet me up at the entry to Applehead Island in an hour or so."

"Will do. See you there."

I entered the Kingsland County Sheriff's Department on my phone, retrieved the address, and drove directly there. It was a large, squat, nondescript building in the north part of the county, set back from the street with a large parking lot in the front. It seemed larger than it should be, and I wondered if it housed a jail. I entered the lobby through a glass door, and directly in my path was a metal detector. I glanced left and noted an officer with a very unfriendly face at a desk.

"State your business."

"I'm Dr. Jim Brady. I'd like to see the sheriff, please."

"He sick?"

"That, I don't know. I'd like to discuss a personal matter with him."

"Have any ID?"

I produced my Texas driver's license and my Texas medical license. I considered asking him if he would like to see my Costco card, but thought better of it.

"Empty your pockets," he said, after perusing my identification cards. He eyed me suspiciously, then looked back and forth between my picture ID and the live person standing in front of him.

I did as told, and even had to remove my boots, since I beeped the first time I went through the metal detector. He escorted me through the lobby and back through a series of office cubicles toward a glassed-in office. I peered right and left looking for Rob Bates, but thankfully he wasn't there.

"Sheriff, hate to bother you, but this man says he's a doctor and wants to speak with you."

The sheriff rose and was the typical movie law-enforcement officer I had come to expect. He was tall and beefy with a large gut and had a wad of chewing tobacco in his cheek.

"Sheriff Holmes," he said, but didn't extend his hand. "Have a seat."

We both sat, and he asked me to state my business. I gave him the story of Rob Bates's abuse of both his wife and his mother-in-law Lucy, including his most recent escapade into HCMC, where in a fit of anger, he attempted to damage my recent repair of Julie's hip. I included Deputy Bates's encounters with me on the two occasions, one witnessed by a security guard at the resort, the other by a Horseshoe Bay police officer at a speed trap.

"Got any witnesses to the physical abuse of the women?"

I had to think for a minute. He had blackened Lucy's eye, shoved Julie into a moving vehicle, and pummeled Julie's hip with his fist. Were there any witnesses to any of these events? I thought not. But I had experienced his abuse to me on two occasions, both times witnessed by others.

"No, but—"

"Sir, I'm sure you mean well, but you can't come in here and accuse one of my deputies of assaults that cannot be corroborated. We face issues of police brutality every day, so without another witness, there is nothing I can do for you."

"I told you about the two men who witnessed his confrontations with me."

"Yes you did, but what I'm hearing is that on the first occasion, Deputy Bates was trying to get some information about his wife, and on the second, he pulled you over for speeding." With that comment, he opened his desk and pulled out a form of some sort and handed it to me.

It was a Kingsland County Sheriff's Department Moving Violation Citation form, with my name on it, and signed by R. Bates, Deputy Sheriff, stating I was doing 80 in a 65 mph zone, and that he had given me a warning and sent me on my way.

"That is you, right, Doc?"

"Yes, but—"

"I think we're done here. The way I see it, Deputy Bates did you a favor, sort of a friendly welcome to our little town. Drive safe, hear?"

And with that, I was escorted out of his office by my original contact at the desk and sent on my way. I again looked for Rob Bates, but his presence was not noted.

I met Mary Louise and Chuck Strauss, the real estate agent, at the gated entry to Applehead Island. It was a beautiful enclave, with houses built up high on the hills having a distant water view, and lake-level homes with boat docks right next to the patios. We looked at a high one and a low one and decided that, while the lake-level homes were nice, and the personal boat dock was convenient, the bugs that thrived on the lake were not welcome visitors. Living high on one of the hills was more our style. The bugs did not thrive at altitude.

We each drove back to the resort. Mary Louise garaged her car while I went up to the apartment and retrieved my retriever. I walked him, then took my wife to dinner at River City Grille. It sat high above a section of the Colorado River called Lake Marble Falls, with outstanding water and sunset views. We dined on fresh oysters and frog legs, added horseradish to the already zesty red sauce, and washed it down with a pitcher of ice-cold Modelo Especial.

We kept to the speed limit of forty-five on the drive back to the apartment and were almost at the exit to the resort when I saw the flashing lights behind me. We had only shared the one pitcher of beer, and fortunately had each downed a caffeinated cola prior to leaving. I wouldn't swear to it, but I thought my blood alcohol would be under the limit. I pulled onto the shoulder, not one hundred yards from the resort entry. So close, and yet so far.

I rolled down my driver's window but kept the motor running.

"License and registration, please," said the officer. The logo on his uniform read Granite Falls police. Only his last name was engraved on the nametag, and it read Beverley.

I handed him my license, then retrieved the registration card and proof of insurance from the console. He perused both, then asked, "Have you been drinking?"

"We had a beer with dinner."

"Do you know why I stopped you, sir?"

"No. I don't think I was speeding."

He leaned down into my window and peered at Mary Louise. "Ma'am," he said.

"Officer," she responded.

He handed me my identification papers.

"I don't know, Doctor, what your long-term plans are. I heard through the grapevine that you performed some pretty amazing surgery on Rob Bates's wife, so we're always indebted to those who come to the aid of a fellow officer's family. Even though he's with the Kingsland County Sheriff's Department, we're all part of the same fellowship, whether it be HSB police, Marble Falls police, or Granite Falls police. That said, I would heed my advice, which is stick to doctoring, and stay out of the private lives of our citizens. I would hate to see someone of your talent, or your beautiful wife, succumb to any unfortunate accidents. And I mean that. I've lived here all my life, and I know these folks much better than you.

"Have a good evening."

CHAPTER 14

INVESTIGATION

The encounter with Officer Beverley prompted a firestorm of controversy between Mary Louise and me. It began with her asking if there was anything I would like to tell her, and after my answering no, she eventually coerced me to confess my visit to Sheriff Holmes about Rob Bates.

"You've really stepped in it this time, Jim Bob. It's one thing to investigate everyday ordinary citizens who might have done something illegal, but to involve yourself against men in law enforcement? That's idiotic!"

"I'd like to point out that Officer Beverley didn't necessarily chastise me, nor did he say he wasn't on my side. He told me to be careful, in so many words. I think it was a warning to look out for certain law officers in the community, not a threat."

We went round and round after that. I wasn't used to verbal battles with Mary Louise. She was quite the debater, though, and she eventually wore me down, discounting my arguments as naive, childish, uninformed, and unsubstantiated. Mostly she feared for my safety, and I had to agree, I *had* stepped in it this time.

I vowed to stay away from Rob Bates, to stick to medicine, and to make up my mind to either play golf and enjoy retirement, return to work in Houston, or take up a position at HCMC and work an abbreviated schedule. I went to bed chastised, like a puppy who had done his business on an Oriental rug.

Next morning, I called J. J. to see if he had discovered any other information about the missing women. It seemed to me that following up on that issue was not aligning myself against law-enforcement personnel. It was a matter of intellectual curiosity.

"Pop, I must say, the one thing these women have in common is that they seem to have nothing in common. I've looked at their lives from routine angles, from schooling, to jobs, to neighborhoods they live in, and to their husbands and their associations, and I came up with zilch. I did, however, find one item, and I don't know what it means. I had to hack into a database I try to stay away from, but when there are no commonalities between people, I get suspicious."

"I didn't intend to get you in trouble. I'm in enough trouble with your mother because of my snooping around, so she would never forgive me if I somehow dragged you down with me."

"Not to worry, Pop. I'm fine. I can hack my way into sites and cover my tracks on the way out. I accessed hospital records in the area and came up with a common thread. All six women had, at one time or another, been patients at Hill Country Medical Center. Each woman had gone to the emergency room with an injury—broken arm, broken nose, fractured ankle, concussion. Some stayed overnight, some went home the same day. And, these injuries tended to be multiple. The least ER usage was twice, the most, six times. Six times! And of course, that got me to thinking about a pattern of spousal abuse."

"Holy shit, son. I feel like I've stepped off into the abyss."

"Well, that's not all. I surmised that since each woman worked, each might have their own checking account. And bingo. After I cross-referenced each woman's name with local banks in your area, I discovered that each woman had a checking account in their name only, and each made a monthly payment via automatic bank draft to a place called Mourning Doves. I found a website called Mourning Doves, but it was locked down tight and impossible to access. However, once I had a notion that the basic issue might be spousal abuse, I started researching various women's websites, and there it was again: Mourning Doves."

"Wow, that's spectacular work, son. I just don't know what I'm going to do about it. I promised your mother I would lay off these investigative escapades of mine and either enjoy retirement or return to work."

"Pops, remember back, years ago, when you got involved in the shooting death of the insurance magnate Paul Thompson, Susan Beeson gave you a badge that made you an investigator with the Houston Police Department?"

"Sure. I had free rein for a while, and it was a gas, man."

"Well, clear it with Mom first, but I think it's time to dust that baby off."

The conversation with J. J. prompted another sit-down discussion with Mary Louise. I convinced her I would steer clear of law enforcement but simply wanted to interview the children, and maybe the husbands, of the missing women. I could guise myself as an HPD investigator, since, after all, I had a badge. Our long-time housekeeper, Tonita, located my old badge back at home in Houston, and via Fed Ex, I had it in one day.

This case of the missing women had presented itself to me. I had not gone looking for a mystery to solve. I had simply tried to help Julie Bates, and as some of my friends say, no good deed goes unpunished. Nonetheless, I was in the thick of the situation and intended to try and see it through. No one else had determined the fate of the missing women, so perhaps it was up to me.

I decided to begin with medical records at Hill Country Medical Center. I walked on water as far as the staff was concerned after repairing Julie Bates's hip, so why not take advantage of the situation? I introduced myself to the medical records clerk, Melanie Scherer, who sat at a desk at the east end of the third floor of the hospital, on the opposite side of the floor from the inpatient wing.

"Morning, Melanie, I'm Dr. Jim Brady," I said, extending my hand.

"Morning, Doctor. I know you by reputation already," she said, shaking my hand. "What can I help you with, sir?"

"I'm looking for the charts on six women who have been in the news as of late. It's my understanding that all of them had been patients here at HCMC prior to their disappearance. I'd like to review their medical records. The first is—"

"Doctor, do you have medical privileges here? And do you have HIPPA consent to review these women's medical records? Because of privacy laws, I can't let just anyone view patients' charts."

"I do not, but all these women have disappeared, and I would think that HIPPA consent would be suspended during a criminal investigation. And yes, I have full privileges here at HCMC."

"Please have a seat, Doctor, and let me call Dr. Owens's office."

I sat, she dialed, we both waited. After a short time, Buck Owens appeared in person. I stood and shook his hand, and he pulled me aside.

"What's going on, Jim?"

"Buck, I realize I should have contacted your office first, and I apologize for not doing so. I wasn't thinking clearly. I have a list of the six women who have disappeared from the area over the past year. I became curious, as I have been known to do, and started to look into the matter, since the local authorities have had no success in locating these women, or finding their remains. My son J. J. has a private investigation firm. He did some research at my request, and he found out that a common thread exists between all six women. Each was a patient here at HCMC and treated for various injuries that could be attributed to spousal abuse. I'd like to look at each woman's medical records, confirm that for myself, and see where it leads me."

At that point, I reached into my jacket pocket and extracted my special-investigator badge.

"What's that, Jim?"

"I am a special investigator with the Houston PD and have all rights and privileges extended to me by this badge. I'm official, if you will, and while I don't want to get crossways with you or the board, I believe that this information I've acquired through my son's company could be of vital importance in discovering what happened to these women. I merely want to review their medical records, confirm that each was a patient here, and review injuries sustained and their outcome."

Buck mulled that over for a bit, walked around the corner to the south wing of the floor, and stared through the wall-sized window at the Texas landscape. He then returned to Melanie's desk.

"Okay, Jim, I'll cut you some slack on this. I've granted you full privileges here, and as a staff member in good standing, you can review pertinent medical records. And you are correct about HIPPA laws being suspended in the course of a criminal investigation regarding these women's disappearance. Melanie, give him what he wants, please."

Buck shook my hand and left the floor. Melanie handed me a request form and a pen. "I assume you'll want copies, Doctor?"

CHAPTER 15

THE WOMEN

I took the six charts, found a cubicle adjacent to medical records, and began my review. I flipped back and forth between the medical records data and J. J.'s information from his research. He had downloaded multiple photographs of each woman—from where, I didn't know, nor did I care to ask. I made notes as I read, and I collated the data as best I could.

Margaret Harris, age 37, disappeared November 12 of last year. She had two prior visits to the HCMC emergency room. The first was in the previous January, the second in May. The first was for a concussion sustained in a fall at home. The second was for a wrist injury, which turned out to be a fracture of the radius bone. The fracture was nondisplaced, requiring a cast but not surgery. The wrist injury was said to have been caused when she tried to break up a dog fight between her pet German shepherd and a neighbor's pit bull. On both occasions, she was brought to the ER by her husband, who was and still is a detective with the Granite Falls Police Department. She was kept overnight for observation after the concussion but was sent home with a cast after the second injury. Her husband was listed as next of kin, and as I remember from J. J.'s review, she had no children.

At the time of both injuries, she was a dispatcher with Big Tex Trucking Company. She had disappeared after leaving work around six in the evening.

Katie Smith, age 52, disappeared January 15. She had six visits to the ER at HCMC over the prior three years, two per year. The first injury recorded was a neck sprain sustained in a one-car accident, when she allegedly swerved off a county road to avoid hitting a stray cow. The second was a fractured ankle sustained in a fall off her front porch the same year, which required a fibular plate and ligament repair. She was admitted overnight. The following year, she sustained two shoulder dislocations five months apart, both due to falls off her horse according to the intake form. Both dislocations were reduced in the ER with sedation. Neither required admission to the hospital. Last year, she had a nasal bone fracture when she slipped on a freshly waxed floor. It was realigned in the ER with sedation and splinted. Admission was not required. Her last recorded visit was also last year, when she presented to the ER with severe abdominal pain and vaginal bleeding. At the time of D&C, she was found to be eight weeks pregnant. She was kept overnight after that procedure.

On all visits except the last, she was accompanied by her husband, a dentist with offices in Marble Falls and Granite Falls. Her sister brought her to the ER for the abdominal problem. Katie had two grown children, one in Austin and one in Dallas. She had worked as an event planner at Hill Country Resort and disappeared around eight thirty in the evening after a function she had planned.

Carla Robinson, age 44, disappeared March 9. She had two visits to the ER. The first was the end of last year, with what turned out to be a fractured rib and a punctured lung. She had fallen off a ladder while cleaning the gutters at home. She was in the hospital for three days, until the lung expanded. She had another visit in early this year for a laceration to the foot. Her Pomeranian had broken off his leash while she was walking him. She was barefoot, and in the process of chasing him down, she stepped on broken glass on a vacant lot across the street. There was no tendon injury, but the laceration required twenty stitches. She did not require hospitalization.

On both occasions, she was brought to the ER by her mother. Her husband was a long-haul trucker who worked for Big Tex and was on the road five days a week. She had worked as a nurse on the three-to-eleven evening shift at HCMC, and disappeared after leaving work around eleven thirty. She had one daughter, in her senior year at Texas State in San Marcos.

Karen Statton, age 48, disappeared in May. She had two visits to the ER, the first in December of last year, for what was called a strep throat. She was given penicillin and sent home. The next visit was in February this year, for a knee injury. She told the ER nurse that "it just popped out." She was diagnosed with a dislocated patella, underwent reduction in the ER, and was sent home in a splint.

She was brought into the ER by her husband on both occasions. He was an engineer at the Ferguson power plant. She worked as a nurse in the ICU at HCMC, on the day shift, seven in the morning to three in the afternoon. She didn't show up for a weekly canasta game scheduled for five o'clock. She had one son, a senior in medical school in Houston.

Jorja Watson, age 39, disappeared July 11. She had one visit to the ER, in February, for an ear injury. She thought she had a bug in her ear and she was trying to clean out the ear with a Q-tip, got too aggressive, and got the Q-tip stuck. When examined, there was no bug in the ear, just some thick ear wax, but her eardrum was punctured. She was not admitted.

Her husband brought her to the ER. They jointly owned a real estate firm, Bay Country Realty. She disappeared around eleven in the morning, after a property showing. She didn't show up for her next appointment. She had no children.

Last was Hilary Allen, age 46, disappeared September 17. She had three visits to the ER, all this year. The first visit was in January for a lumbar spinal-process fracture that occurred after a fall. While it's a painful injury, that segment of the bone does not contribute to stability, so she was discharged. The next two visits occurred in February, one week apart, for persistent pain in the lumbar spine. X-rays showed delayed healing of the fracture. She was again discharged.

Her sister brought her to the ER on all three occasions. Hilary was vice president of Lake Savings and Trust and disappeared after a business lunch at Forno's. She had three children: one in law school, one a senior in college, and one working as a teller at Lake Savings and Trust. Her husband was a litigation lawyer in Austin and came home on weekends.

After reviewing the missing women's medical records, there was no glaring evidence of spousal abuse. The illnesses and injuries I reviewed could have occurred exactly as the women said in their intake interviews. And nothing in the medical records provided any clue whatsoever as to the cause of any of the women's disappearance. Each of their appearances in the ER could be explained by the fact that HCMC is the largest and closest hospital facility in the Highland Lakes area. It could have been a matter of convenience.

I searched the internet for hospital facilities and urgent-care clinics in the area. There were small hospitals in Llano and Burnet, and urgent-care clinics in Marble Falls, Llano, and Burnet. These women had other choices, but they selected HCMC. Two of the women worked as nurses at this facility, so I could understand their choosing their place of employment for medical care. The other four women could have been treated elsewhere. What did any of this mean?

I called Mary Louise and volunteered to drive her to Austin for a late lunch at a sushi restaurant she loved in the Galleria mall. There was a movie theater next door, and maybe something was showing she would like to see. That would be termed a peace offering. She accepted, and we arrived in under an hour, thanks to light traffic on Highway 71. We had a nice lunch of tekka maki, kappa maki, California roll, hamachi, and white tuna, washed down with Asahi beer.

We walked next door and saw that the remake of *A Star Is Born* was starting in forty-five minutes. We decided to take a stroll around the plaza and happened to walk into a women's clothing store called Chico's. Mary Louise selected a pashmina scarf she liked, modeled it in front of a mirror, and gave it five stars. A pleasant woman was stationed at the checkout counter, and she took our credit card and wrapped the scarf as though it was a gift. Her eyes met mine, and she looked very familiar. I smiled, she smiled.

"You look so familiar. Do we know each other?" I asked.

"No sir, I don't think so. People say that to me all the time. I guess I have one of those faces. Y'all have a nice day."

We strolled back toward the theater and saw the show. It was very good, and I especially enjoyed the music. Lady Gaga and Bradley Cooper were quite a duo on-screen, but what sadness there was in their movie relationship. However, I couldn't stop thinking about the clerk at Chico's. She obviously had a striking resemblance to someone I knew but whose name I couldn't remember.

It was dark by the time we returned home. I unloaded my collection of documents, went upstairs and fetched Tip, and took him for a walk while Mary Louise went about her nightly bathroom routine. We retired early, tired from the day's activities. I woke up at three in the morning, startled by some dream I couldn't remember. I went into the kitchen for a glass of water and noticed the documents lying on the dining room table. I opened the file and found myself staring at the face of the store clerk. It was the face of Margaret Harris, one of the missing women.

CHAPTER 16

ROBERT ALLEN

I couldn't get back to sleep, so I finally arose at five and made a pot of coffee. While the brew dripped, I studied Margaret Harris's photographs. Her face was shown from several different angles. This Margaret had longish brown hair, brown eyes, a medium-sized nose, and a few more frown lines than would be expected on a thirty-seven-year-old woman. The store clerk had blond hair cut short, blue eyes, a small nose, and a virtually wrinkle-free face. But I could see the resemblance in the facial bone structure.

Were the two women one and the same, or was it a coincidental likeness between two strangers, like a doppelganger? I've read that everyone has a twin somewhere.

"Morning," Mary Louise offered. She was lovely in the morning, with her sleepy eyes, perfectly tousled hair, and sweet demeanor.

"Morning. Coffee?"

"Please. Why are you up so early?"

"I spent yesterday at medical records at HCMC, reviewing hospital ER visits by the six women that disappeared. Did I mention to you that J. J. found that all six had been patients at the hospital?"

"Yes, after your call with him."

"I collated the files and photographs J. J. sent me with info I gleaned from an exhaustive study of the various pertinent medical records. What do you think?"

I laid out several photos of Margaret Harris. "This is the first missing woman."

She looked at each carefully. "She looks familiar."

"I agree. Remember the clerk at Chico's yesterday? Do they bear a resemblance?"

She studied the photos again, closer and more carefully. "Yes, very much so."

"That's what I thought. I'm tempted to go back there today and take another look at her. What if *she's* Margaret Harris? That would certainly solve a mystery."

"I agree, but what are the chances? This woman has been missing for what, a year? And she shows up after all that time as a clerk in a store fifty miles from where she disappeared? I mean, if you are thinking she's a runaway, why would she stay in an area where she could be recognized? I'm sure there have been many people from this area who have shopped at the Galleria mall. If I was running from something, I'd get as far away as I could. I realize that would be an easy solution to her disappearance, but that doesn't ring true for me. A resemblance doesn't mean the two women are one and the same."

She was right. A silly thought. I needed to keep digging.

"What are you doing today?" she asked.

"I don't know yet. I'm mulling things over. You?"

"I'm going back to bed. Care to join me?"

I was a little late walking and feeding Tip, and I could sense his annoyance. I'm sure it didn't help his hurt feelings when I told him a man's gotta do what a man's gotta do.

I sat on the terrace, drank more coffee, and reviewed my notes. Mary Louise had gone back to sleep. Where was I going with all this missing-women business? What did I think I could do that the authorities couldn't? I had no real credentials, no official status. I was just a doctor on a sabbatical from his job, playing hooky, if you will. I was neglecting patients that I could actually do something for, something that I was trained to do and was good at. But there was this unspoken draw for me to stay here in the Hill Country— to accomplish exactly what, I didn't know. I wondered if there was some cosmic force silently imploring me to remain here and do something, find out something, do some good in a fashion I wasn't yet aware of. Or maybe I was just a tired old surgeon who had seen his better days, ready to be put out to pasture but holding on for dear life with both hands to some intrinsic value from the bygone past.

And yet I trudged on.

I wanted to talk to each husband but thought that might become a problem if these cases of missing women had anything to do with spousal abuse. It occurred to me that the children of the women involved might be more receptive to discussing their mothers with me. I reviewed the documents from medical records at HCMC and reminded myself that none of the children of these women had accompanied them to the emergency room. That was easily explained by the fact that all except one lived in other cities. Fortunately, the extensive review that J. J. had performed included names, addresses, and phone numbers of all the parties involved, including the offspring of the victims.

Hilary Allen's oldest son, Robert Allen, worked at Lake Savings and Trust. I called his cell number but did not speak to a live person. The voice-mail prompt instructed me to leave a message, which I did.

"Robert, my name is Dr. Jim Brady, and I'm looking into your mother's disappearance. I'd like to speak to you this afternoon after work and wondered if it would be convenient to meet me for a drink at the bar patio at On the Rocks between five and six. Let me know," and I gave him my cell number.

I showered and dressed and took Tip for a walk. Upon my return, Mary Louise informed me that she was screening properties today, choosing the ones she thought I would like, and that we could meet for a late lunch if I was available. We would text each other about the time. I kissed her, patted Tip on his fat head, and headed to Hill Country Medical Center.

Julie Bates wasn't in her bed in the rehab unit when I arrived. I inquired as to her location with the ward clerk, and she directed me to the physical therapy facility on the first floor. When I arrived there, I spotted Julie on a walker, assisted by a therapist.

"Morning, Julie. How's the hip?"

"Much better, thanks." I had the therapist direct her to a private exam room, where I had her lay down, and I examined the incisional area.

"Well, there is quite a bit of bruising, but no signs of infection or disruption of the tissues."

I put her hip through a full range of motion, and that caused no pain.

"I think you're fine, Julie. How much longer in the rehab unit?"

"I'm approved for one more week, Dr. Brady. Then I'm out of here."

"Where will you go when you leave?"

"Back to Mom's."

"Will you be safe there?"

"As safe as I've always been."

With that, I bid her a good morning and made the trek down to Dr. Buck Owens's office.

"Morning, Lucy," I said.

"Morning, Dr. Brady. Did you see Julie?"

"I did, and she's looking pretty good. She has another week in rehab, she told me, then she's going back to your house."

"Yes, she is. Hopefully I can keep her safe."

"I hope so too. You'll be working, so she'll be alone most of the day. I wonder how long it will be before she can return to her radiology technician job? At least if she's at work, she's fairly safe."

"She thinks a couple of weeks, although she won't be able to do the procedures she would normally assist in. That will take a while. She obviously wants to get back to work as soon as possible."

"This business with her abusive husband, that's been going on a long time, I guess?"

"Yes, sir. Julie keeps thinking he'll change, and he continues to promise her that he will, but then something triggers this anger inside him and he's out of control. We have to walk on eggshells around him."

"I'm no expert in these matters, but that seems like a horrible way to live."

"It is. If she hadn't been in that accident, she . . ."

"She what, Lucy?"

"Oh, never you mind. You have much more important matters to deal with. Are you looking for Dr. Owens?"

"Yes I am, but I'm not sure I have anything more important to do than look out for your daughter's safety. Is he in?"

"No sir, he's at an off-campus meeting. Can I give him a message?"

"No thanks, I just wanted to offer him an apology for getting those medical records on the six missing women without his permission. Sometimes I'm like a bull in a china closet, and I act before I think."

She stood, extended her hand, gripped mine tightly. "We're glad you did. All of us."

When I returned to my car, I noticed I had a message on the cell phone. It was from Robert Allen, confirming he was available to meet me at five thirty for a drink. He was puzzled about my involvement in his mother's disappearance, since he had never heard of me and had no idea what I was doing poking around in family business. I decided not to answer that message but would simply show up at the scheduled meeting place. I could answer his questions then.

I met Mary Louise at Waterfront, a seafood restaurant on the shores of Lake LBJ. We selected a shared dish, a potpourri of fresh seafood with shrimp, crab, catfish, sausage, and hush puppies. She opted for the grilled items, while I took charge of the fried food. For a change, we both had sweet iced tea for a beverage. I assumed we were giving our livers a brief respite from trauma.

Afterward, she continued on with her search for property, and I returned home to walk Tip. I shuffled through the paperwork on the missing women, reviewed the segment on Hilary Allen, then headed back out to On the Rocks.

I chose a table outside, high above the Colorado River and Lake LBJ, ordered a beer, and waited. After a half hour or so, a tall young man dressed in a business suit stepped onto the patio, looked around, and approached my table. "Are you Dr. Brady?"

"I am," standing to shake his hand. "Have a seat. Beverage?"

"Yes, please."

Robert was over six feet tall, in his twenties, with black hair combed straight back but almost shaved over his ears, dark eyebrows and eyes, thin lips, and a fashionable five o'clock shadow.

I motioned the server over, and she took his order for a Hendricks gin martini, up, with onions.

"Thanks for meeting me. I'm an orthopedic surgeon from Houston, on sabbatical and looking to make some changes in my life, and I stumbled across this mystery of six missing women from the area. I have functioned as a special investigator in the past for several cases in Houston and have some experience and expertise in solving crimes or mysteries that went neglected. I have a badge, if you'd like some proof."

"That won't be necessary. There is word around town already about you, so I checked you out after you called me. It's a very small community, especially when it comes to gossip."

His drink came. We clinked glasses.

"Your mother vanished after a business lunch at Forno's, from what I gather from the records I reviewed."

"Yes. She met a potential banking client at twelve-thirty and hasn't been heard from since. It's been three months."

"Do you have any thoughts about what happened to her?"

He sighed. "Mom was a trusting sort, thought the best of everyone, so she could have met with a fateful end by a total stranger. I don't know. She and Dad . . . well, they had their problems."

"Was there any history between them of, how shall I put it, violence?"

"Yes, but that was in the past."

"Did you know any of the other missing women or their families?"

"No."

"According to the ER records at Hill Country Medical Center, she came into the hospital with a spinal injury. She had fallen and fractured a spinous process. It's a painful injury but not one that requires surgery to restore stability. It would take a pretty hard fall to break one of those off. Do you know anything about that?"

"Very little. Her sister took her in when it happened."

"She went back to the ER twice for persistent pain. The ER records state that the fracture wasn't healing."

"That's what I understand."

"Nothing else you can share with me, Robert?"

"Sorry. You know, I'm working here only temporarily. I'd like to get back to Austin as soon as possible. My sister is in law school there, and my brother is a college senior and has applied to law school. I'm the only black-sheep banker in the family. My dad's a lawyer also. His practice is in Austin. He goes home on the weekends."

"Why didn't you take a job in Austin after graduation?"

"I had shitty grades. Mom insisted I return here and work in her bank for a while, get some experience, and then re-apply to the larger Austin banks."

"Well, Robert, I'm sorry about your mother. She, like the other five women, disappeared without a trace. The authorities seem to have given up on finding out what happened. I'm working in the dark, to some degree. If there is anything else you think of that might give me some direction, please contact me."

We both stood. He shook my hand, thanked me for my efforts, and left.

CHAPTER 17

LUNCH

Mary Louise wanted to stay in for dinner, so we met at Bay Market and shopped for Italian food—prosciutto, salami, sausages, cheeses—and a loaf of fresh bread with garlic butter. We also bought a Caesar salad and a couple of bottles of pinot noir.

We met back at the apartment. I walked Tip while she prepared dinner.

Over salad, she asked, "How was your day?"

"Unproductive at best."

"Potential crimes went unsolved?"

"For sure. How about you? Find us a home you like?"

"Yes, as a matter of fact. I'd like you to see them tomorrow, if you're available."

"Mary Louise, there is nothing on my plate except wishing and hoping."

She laughed. "I told Chuck we could meet him at ten in the morning."

"That's fine. I plan to contact the offspring of the other four people, see if they have anything important to say. I hope they are more helpful than Robert Allen, Hilary's oldest son."

"He wasn't helpful?"

"He basically said he knew nothing, which I find hard to believe. He did admit there was some sort of spousal abuse going on in the home, but he said it was in the past."

"You may remember that I served on the board of the women's center, and for a while volunteered on the hotline for women trying to be rescued. This issue is a very slippery slope, Jim Bob. Families don't want to talk about it, women don't want to admit to it. Many women you come in contact with are in desperate situations and are running for their lives. It's a horrible problem, and much more common than our society would like to admit."

"Have you ever heard of a group called Mourning Doves?"

"How did you hear of them?" she asked, with a strange look on her face.

"J.J. came across the name when he was researching bank accounts of the missing women. He told me that each woman that disappeared had a job, and had her own checking account, and that in each case, there was a monthly automatic payment to Mourning Doves."

She sighed. "It's an organization for women who are victims of domestic violence. They specialize in offering services to abused women, such as protection, counseling, and legal advice. Their main focus, however, is escape, or so I was told when I was active on the hotline."

"What do you mean by escape?"

"Exactly that. Escape from the domestic violence situation. Possibly a disappearance, if you will. A new life."

I tossed and turned that night, thinking about Mourning Doves and now wondering if these missing women had escaped into a new life, rather than having met with a violent end. Now I really wanted to return to Chico's in Austin and speak to the store clerk, not that she would be forthcoming about her past history.

But Mary Louise was right. If she was a runaway, why go to the trouble of disappearing, only to go to work at a clothing store less than an hour away from where the abuse had occurred?

And I then wondered about the offspring of the missing women. If the mothers had disappeared to escape spousal abuse, wouldn't the kids know? I can't imagine Robert Allen not knowing if his mother had escaped into another life. I could see him not wanting to confide in me, a stranger, but how could a mother leave her grown children behind with no idea of what had happened to her? There had to be a deep, dark secret involved in this mystery. I needed more information, but I had to be careful. If six women had disappeared to escape domestic abuse, then these spouses were capable of violence toward anyone, yours truly especially, who was poking at rattlesnakes.

I left messages with all the other children of the missing women. Neither Margaret Harris nor Jorja Watson had kids. Katie Smith had a daughter in Dallas and a son in Austin. Carla Robinson had a daughter, a senior at Texas State in San Marcos. Karen Statton had a son, a senior in medical school in Houston. Hilary Allen had two offspring in addition to Robert, as he'd mentioned during our meeting. That was six calls to be returned. My expectations were low.

We met real estate agent Chuck at a beautiful home overlooking Lake LBJ. It was high enough to have an expansive view of the water and the surrounding Texas Hill Country, but not close enough to the water to attract insects. The residence was in a gated community with only five other homes. From the front, the house appeared narrow, but upon entry, the layout was pie-shaped, with an expansive open living area. There was a walk-in bar to the left, a great room in the center, and a dining room to the right. We walked out onto the deck and appreciated the eastern view. A western, or sunset, view sounds attractive, but in Texas, it's just too hot.

The master bedroom had excellent views as well, with his-and-her clothes closets and his-and-hers water closets. The tub and shower would have to be shared. That worked for me. Hope springs eternal.

The listing agent introduced himself as James Watson. He left the showing to Chuck, our agent, but I'm sure he wanted us to know he would be sharing the commission if we bought the house. He wasn't particularly friendly, and I wondered if he was any relation to Jorja Watson, one of the missing women. I wanted to ask but thought better of it.

There were two more bedrooms upstairs, each with its own bath and balcony, and with expansive views of the lake.

As far as I could tell, the house was perfect for our needs, should we relocate to Granite Falls. That decision hadn't been made yet, so we left and viewed two similar properties, Mary Louise and I are both a little afraid of making a real estate commitment because of my indecision regarding my career. I really did like that first house, though, and would hate to lose it.

Chuck wanted to take us to lunch, so we drove into Marble Falls and ate at the Blue Bonnet Cafe. Over a lunch of fried chicken and fried shrimp, we discussed prices, closing dates, and other unpleasant necessities of home buying. I casually asked him if James Watson happened to be related to Jorja Watson. He stopped eating and stared at me.

"Why would you ask me that?"

"Why wouldn't I? Is that sacred ground?"

"Well, no, but his wife went missing, what, four or five months ago? I imagine he's suffering."

I looked at Mary Louise, puzzled. "Is it off limits to discuss the disappearance of a woman who hasn't been found, either alive or dead?"

"I guess not; just seems a little insensitive to me."

"So, he and the other husbands would rather suffer than share any information that might be helpful in discovering what happened to their wives?"

"Jim, might I ask what business this is of yours? You're a surgeon that the hospital is trying to recruit to come and work here. You're not here on police business."

"I'm looking into the matter. I have special-investigator status with the Houston Police Department and approval from Buck Owens, and my son, who has a private investigation company, and I have partnered up and are looking into these disappearances. I guess you could say I have no business interfering in the investigation, but as far as I can tell, the search for answers in these cases is stalled. I don't think anyone is actively pursuing the matter. The last disappearance was only three months ago, and I don't see any news on the front page of the local paper."

"I'm sorry, you are right. I've heard some rumors that you were reviewing the missing-women cases, and some of us, well, just don't understand why you're involved. You don't even live here."

"You know, Chuck, when I am confronted with an unanswered question, I try and find an answer. That's just the way I'm wired."

I wanted to launch a tirade about possible spousal abuse and domestic violence, but I thought it best to leave that subject alone for now. If word got out that I was focusing on that issue, all potential doors would probably shut.

We thanked Chuck for lunch and told him we would be in touch.

I checked my phone for messages from my calls to the six offspring of the missing women, but there were no responses.

I felt I had neglected an integral part of my so-called investigation, and that was to discuss my findings and suspicions with the chief of police of one of the local cities, either Marble Falls, Granite Falls, or Horseshoe Bay. I chose Granite Falls. Mary Louise and I went back to the apartment, and I gathered up all the documents and headed to the police station. She assured me that Tip would receive a proper walk in my absence.

CHAPTER 18

CHIEF FERTITTA

The Granite Falls Police Department was a short drive from the HCMC. It was housed in a modern white stucco one-story building similar to the sheriff's office in Kingsland County. Upon entering, however, I appreciated that there was no metal detector at the central entry. I saw one in the distance, in front of an entry to another area. There was an elevated desk on the left, where sat a uniformed officer. He had sergeant's stripes on his sleeves. His nameplate read McCready.

"Afternoon, sir, I'm Dr. Jim Brady. I'd like to see the police chief, please."

"And I'd like to see Pope Francis, Doctor, but that probably isn't going to happen. What business do you have with the chief?"

"Well, truth be known, I'd like to share some information I've gleaned about the missing-women cases. I thought he would be interested."

He stared at me for a moment. "And how would you be obtaining this information? You said you were a doctor? What kind of doctor?"

"Orthopedic surgeon, in Houston, but I'm here looking at a job at Hill Country Medical Center."

"I don't understand the relationship between doctoring and having information about the disappearances."

"I would be happy to discuss that with the police chief."

He exhaled in a frustrated manner. "Wait here."

I sat in a small waiting area, along with four other folks. I wondered if these were loved ones of the jailed accused. I then wondered if there was a jail here. With that metal detector, there could be.

Sgt. McCready returned and motioned to me to follow him. I knew the routine, so I emptied my pockets, including my badge in case I had to resort to that, removed my boots, and passed through. We walked down a hallway, at the end of which was a cell door, beyond which I could hear the catcalls of the inmates. We veered off to the right, walked through a series of offices with cubicles, then entered a conference room.

"Have a seat," he said.

Ten or fifteen minutes passed, then a swarthy man entered, about five foot eight inches, bald, with a mustache and the requisite uniform.

"Chief Fertitta," he said, extending his hand. "What can I do for you?"

"Dr. Jim Brady. I'm an orthopedic surgeon from Houston, looking at a position at HCMC. I have some information I wanted to share with you."

"Do you know why you're sitting here in our conference room? Because when McCready gave me some background on you, I called my old friend Stan Lombardo, retired Houston police chief, and got the skinny on you. He says you're a royal pain in the ass, a halfway decent surgeon—and by the way, his hip still hurts—and a pretty fair investigator of various crimes. Seems he worked with you when he was chief, and more recently, his daughter Susan Beeson, current police chief, has worked with you as well. He recommended I at least hear what you have to say."

To quote that old adage, I'd rather be lucky than good. I had three choices of police stations and picked the one where the chief of police knew my old friend Stan Lombardo. That paved the way for my entry.

"Glad to hear Stan is doing well. How do you know each other?"

"We both grew up in Galveston, both from old Italian American families. Stan is a few years older than me, was best friends with my older brother. After the service, Stan ended up in Houston, and I came to the Lake LBJ area. I was done with humidity, mosquitos, and hurricanes. I was an MP in the army and got a taste for police work. One thing led to another, and here I am, police chief of Granite Falls. I'll be retiring in the not-too-distant future, so you might want to share your information with me before they take away my badge."

I shared with Chief Fertitta the names of the missing women, their children, their husbands, their places of employment, their various visits to the ER at HCMC, and J. J.'s findings regarding their contributions to Mourning Doves.

"Jim, I must say, this is very informative, especially categorizing the data in this fashion. You know, when these disappearances started back last year, the law enforcement agencies in the area all started sharing their data. That included our office, Marble Falls police, Horseshoe Bay police, and Kingsland, Llano, and Burnet County police and sheriff's offices. We didn't collate the data to the extent you have, so I'm impressed. Did you know that after the third woman went missing, we called in the FBI? They sent a profiler down here, a nice young woman with unfortunately not much experience. We had no evidence of a crime committed by any of the family members, husbands included. The women simply were here and working one day, and the next day, gone. The profiler concluded that based on the previous timing of a disappearance every two months, we should have another one in November, which as far I know, we didn't. This is December, so the window for some sort of pattern crime has ended. All the agencies are at a loss.

"And now you come in here, with this Mourning Dove business, suggesting that these women were possible victims of spousal abuse, or domestic violence of some sort. Do you have any evidence, other than the monthly contributions to a women's help center of some sort?"

"Absolutely nothing. Just a hunch that I'd like to follow through with."

"Jim, I appreciate your interest in our little part of heaven on the lake, and I certainly would support your decision to come work here and ply your trade. Since we cannot prove there was a crime involved in these disappearances, and since the investigation has stalled and it's not really a police matter, I can't prevent you from going about your business looking into this matter. However, I've been here a long time, and there are, like in any other city, unsavory types that wouldn't hesitate to come after you if you start digging up too much dirt. I would encourage you to tread lightly when looking into domestic violence situation in these homes. It's a hornet's nest, and you can get stung. Badly."

I thanked him for his time and decided to head home. I checked my phone, but still no messages from the sons and daughters of the missing women.

When I entered the apartment, I felt something was amiss. There were two travel suitcases sitting by the front door. Tip was lying on the floor next to the bags. His head was between his legs. He briefly raised up for a pet, then laid his head back down. I heard the clack of Mary Louise's heels on the floor coming around the corner from the master bedroom.

"Where are we going?" I asked sweetly.

"I'm going back to Houston, Jim Bob. You don't seem to have any interest in looking at the homes I've selected. You don't want, or can't, make a decision about what you're going to do with your life. You are in limbo, and I think focusing on these disappearances is an effort to avoid making any long-term decisions. Don't get me wrong, I'm sympathetic to the families of the women, especially the children, regardless of their ages. I've tried to convince you to let the authorities handle the problem. But even after two confrontations with the husband of the woman whose hip you fixed, you doggedly trudge on, with little or no regard to your safety, much less mine.

"I'm taking Tip with me for comfort and security, and also because I don't want him sitting here alone all day while you're out playing detective. I love you with all my heart, and I haven't often involved myself in this investigative hobby of yours, but now that physical danger is a clear risk, I'm taking myself out of the situation. That's what you should be doing as well, but that stubborn streak of yours has taken over, and all sense of reason has disappeared, just like those missing women.

"If you want to come home, I'll be awaiting you with open arms. If you want to move here, and work at the hospital, and stay out of other people's non-medical business and problems, I'll return and stand by your side. But I can't do THIS any longer."

With that, she leashed Tip and tried to handle both rolling suitcases.

"Let me help with—"

"I've got it, thank you. Goodbye."

And with that, she was out the door and gone.

CHAPTER 19

ON MY OWN

Having a cross word with Mary Louise was so rare that I didn't quite know what to do. I should have implored her to stay or offered to give up my search for answers to the missing-women mystery and returned to Houston with her. But I did not. It was like I was paralyzed. I couldn't speak, and I couldn't move. Once she left, I was beside myself. I poured a large single-malt Macallan scotch, added an ice cube, and sat on the terrace and sulked. The sun was going down, and darkness was soon to take over. I was alone—no wife, no dog, only my thoughts to keep me company.

I poured myself another drink. The first one went down way too easily. As I was resuming my position in the outdoor recliner, my phone rang. I hoped it was Mary Louise, returning to me, having changed her mind once she was on the road. But no. I didn't recognize the number but answered it anyway. I would feel better if I could cuss out a telemarketer.

"Dr. Brady here."

"Dr. Brady, my name is Deborah Smith. Katie Smith's daughter. You called me?"

"Yes, thank you for returning my call."

"What is your business with my mother?"

I gave her the background story: orthopedic surgeon, part-time investigator, yada, yada, yada. "I got involved in this business through Lucy Williams, Dr. Buck Owens's assistant. I repaired her daughter Julie's broken hip and pelvis, and one thing led to another. I have a file on your mother's disappearance. She worked in hospitality here at Hill Country Resort as an event planner, and after an event she held the evening of January 15, she was not seen again. Is there anything you can add?"

"No, sir. That's about all I know."

"She obviously hasn't been in touch with you?"

"No."

"Would you have any idea why she might choose to disappear, assuming foul play was not involved?"

She hesitated. "You're thinking Mom might have just left, with no words to us, and went off to another life?"

"I don't know. I'm searching for answers."

"Well, she and Daddy had their differences from time to time, but I can't see that she would disappear from our lives for that."

"I have a record of six visits she made to the ER at Hill Country Medical Center for various fractures. Do you know anything about that?"

"Well, my brother and I used to joke about what a klutz Mom was. I remember some injuries in the past, but I've been out of the house for a while. I live in Dallas now, moved here after college."

"Your mom had two visits to the ER three years ago, the first for a neck injury in a one-car accident, the second for a fractured ankle that required surgery. Two years ago she had two shoulder dislocations, both reduced in the ER with sedation. Last year she had a nasal fracture after slipping on a wet floor, and later had a D&C for vaginal bleeding. Turned out she was eight weeks pregnant. Do you know about any of these injuries?"

The line was silent for a time. "I remember the broken ankle. I came home for a week or so and took care of her. The others I don't know anything about. I can't believe Mom was pregnant, though. She's fifty-two years old."

"What do you do, Deborah?"

"I'm head of the insurance department at Baylor Scott & White hospital. The main hospital and office is in Dallas."

"That sounds like a pretty big job."

"I started as an accountant. Then I worked my way up the ladder, got my CPA credentials and eventually was promoted to my current position. I love working for BSW, and I really enjoy living in Dallas."

"Deborah, thanks much for calling. If there is anything else you can think of that might help me find out what happened to your mother, please let me know."

"I most certainly will, Dr. Brady, and thank you for caring enough about Mom to investigate her disappearance. You didn't even know her."

Reflecting on my conversation with Deborah Harris, I thought her affect was off somewhat. It's like she was taking happy pills. She loved her job at Baylor Scott & White, but she seemed hardly concerned about her missing mother. She could have been the victim of a violent crime, and her corpse could be rotting away in a shallow grave, but Deborah was just so happy to be in Dallas. It's almost as though she knew her mother was all right, although how could she?

And thinking back on my conversation with Robert Allen, he seemed to be oblivious to any pain from his parental loss. He wanted to get back to Austin as soon as possible and work in a larger bank.

Six women, two without kids, four with six kids total. I would like to get a response from the remaining four. I scratched Deborah Smith and Robert Allen off my list of calls to be returned. That left Bill Smith, Deborah's brother, who lived in Austin; Tom Statton, Karen's son and a medical student in Houston; and Alice Allen, in law school in Austin, and David Allen, a senior at the University of Texas, both children of Hilary Allen.

I checked my phone once again for messages, but nothing.

I called Mary Louise on her cell phone to make sure she had arrived home safely. Yes, she had, and thanks for checking in on her. She hoped to see me soon and hung up.

Next morning, I called Cap Rock and asked if there were any tee times available on any of the golf courses. There were, but in the afternoon. I selected one o'clock, took a shower, dressed in my golf clothes, and headed to Austin. There should be plenty of time to make the round trip and be on time for golf.

I found a parking spot close to Chico's, entered the store, and greeted a different salesperson.

"Good morning," I said. "My wife and I were here a couple of days ago and purchased a pashmina scarf in black and gray. Do you have that same scarf in a different color combination?"

"Let's look," she said, and we strode over to the rack and counter where the scarves and shawls were. She pulled out a couple of choices, red and gray, and black and cream. They looked good to me, so I took both.

"There was a blond woman working here the other day. She looked familiar to me, and I thought she might be a long-lost cousin," I lied. "Do you know who I'm talking about?"

"That's Wanda. She's off today."

"I forgot her last name?"

"Jackson," the clerk said.

"That's right. Wanda Jackson. Has she been working here a while?"

"A few months." She ran the credit card, wrapped the scarves in paper, bagged them, and bid me a good day.

That was an expensive method of finding out the name of Margaret Harris's potential twin. My plan was to have J. J. search his sources and see what turned up.

I called J. J. from the car and requested his help in running a background check on Wanda Jackson. I had no idea what would turn up, but I didn't feel comfortable continuing to visit the store, in case Wanda Jackson was really Margaret Harris and felt the need to disappear because of my suspicious actions. But, as Mary Louise told me, it was highly unlikely that a runaway wife would return to an area an hour away from whatever trouble she was running from.

My involvement in these missing women was giving me a splitting headache.

I made my tee time with plenty of time to spare. Apple Rock was a beautiful golf course with rolling hills and enough water to make it interesting. I wasn't paired with anyone, and there were no visible golfers in front of me, so I was able to play in three and one-half hours. During that time, I was able to detach myself from thoughts of disappearing women.

After golf, I stopped by the hospital and checked on Julie Bates. She was back in the rehab ward after physical therapy and was dozing. I was debating on whether to wake her, when a voice startled me.

"She's going home this weekend," said Deputy Sheriff Rob Bates.

I stepped away from him, malevolent ass that he was. "Her wound looks like it's healed well, in spite of your meddling in her recovery."

"What's that supposed to mean?"

"She told her mother and me about your early morning visit, about the pounding you gave her in the incisional area."

"She's lying. She probably did that to herself to get attention. Any witnesses to my so-called visit?"

Of course there weren't, but I was silent about that.

"Just what I suspected. More lies about me. I'm getting tired of that. Things were fine here before you showed up."

"Really? Then why did she leave you and go live with her mother? That happened long before I repaired her hip."

He took a step closer, but the nurse on duty stepped into the room. "How is she, Doc?"

"I haven't examined her yet. I was answering questions from Mr. Bates here."

She looked at him, grimaced, and said, "Maybe it's time to leave now, Rob."

"I'm here visiting my wife. I'm her husband and I have a right to see how she's doing."

"Well, you've seen her, and she's doing fine. So please, let the doctor examine her hip."

He glared at me, turned, and walked away.

"That guy's trouble," I said.

"With a capital T," the nurse answered.

I examined the hip. There was a full range of motion, with no "hitches." Julie woke up while I was evaluating the extremity. "How is it?" she asked.

"Feels good. Your incision is healed well. No more bruising. I think you're ready for the next step."

"I'm a little afraid to go home—Mom's, that is. Did I hear Rob's voice?"

"You did."

"What did he want?"

"To see how you were, he said. That guy makes me very nervous, Julie."

"That's understandable. I feel the same way. I think you should have security walk with you to your car, just to be safe. You never know about him."

"I'll think about that," not wanting to be a wuss or a scared rabbit.

I bid her and the nurse a good evening.

Once in the lobby, I stopped by the security desk and asked for an escort to my car. The trip was uneventful.

By then, I was starving and drove to the yacht club for dinner. I had a Tito's vodka martini, followed by a sliced flank steak with seasonal vegetables. As it turns out, it was the season for broccoli and carrots. I was beginning to miss Mary Louise terribly and realize the error of my ways. I downed another martini for dessert and was getting ready to head home when Buck Owens sat at my bar table.

"Evening, Jim. How goes it?"

"Fair, Buck. I'm growing weary of the investigator's life and ready to do something that has immediate results, like operating on people."

He laughed. "It just so happens that one of our surgeons has a tough case tomorrow and wondered if you'd be able to assist him in surgery."

"What kind of case is it?"

"Spinal decompression and fusion from L1 to S1."

"That's a five-level fusion! That's a rare requirement."

"Patient has adult scoliosis. The surgeon's assistant had a death in the family and had to leave town, so he's desperate. If you aren't available, the doc will have to cancel the case. The family has made a lot of arrangements to accommodate the recovery, so you would be doing all of us a big favor."

"What time is the case scheduled?"

"Seven in the morning."

"Okay, I'll be there. Thanks, Buck."

"You might want to have some coffee," he said, as he walked away.

CHAPTER 20

REUNION

I got up at five, showered and shaved, had some coffee, and arrived at the hospital at 6:15. In the pre-op area, I introduced myself to the patient and his family, telling them I would be assisting in the surgery. They were grateful I had time to help out the surgeon on such short notice. If they only knew how much time I had . . .

The surgery took five hours, but when it was done, I assessed the work as stunningly good. Brad Barkley was a talented spine surgeon. I learned during the case that he was based out of Austin but was spending a couple of days a week in the area seeing patients and operating on those that chose to have their surgery at HCMC instead of Austin, provided the hospital had the appropriate staffing and equipment. He said that HCMC had spared no expense in purchasing equipment for his procedures. He enjoyed the small-town environment and amenities and could see himself practicing here full time, eventually.

Getting my hands back into repairing an orthopedic problem was, in a word, exhilarating. That five hours taught me more about myself than I cared to imagine. Patients might need me, but I needed them more. I knew what my next step was.

I called Mary Louise from the car, telling her I was headed home to get her and my dog and move us to Granite Falls. I was going to work at Hill Country Medical Center, and she might want to put our high-rise apartment in Houston on the market.

I called Buck Owens and told him I was "IN," details to follow.

I was greeted at the door of our Houston home by a freshly groomed Tip, with a western scarf around his thick neck. He stood on his hind legs and let me massage his sweet face with a hand on each side. Just behind him was a freshly groomed Mary Louise, new color on her fingernails and toenails, blond hair up in a "do." She wore tight black leggings with red heels, and a tight matching red sweater. She gently moved Tip aside, put both arms around my neck, and gave me a deep, lingering kiss. We hurried into the master bedroom and could not get our clothes off fast enough.

Afterward, we laid in bed, Tip at our feet. She said, "Welcome home. I know it's only been a few days, but I missed you terribly. I was really worried that you might have lost your desire for me."

"I'm sorry to have given you that impression. As you can see, I will not lose my desire for you. I haven't been thinking clearly, as you know. The issue of the missing women got into my head, and I could honestly think of nothing else. Part of the problem is that no one seems to care about them, and therefore no one seems to be looking for them. Even the two grown children that I talked to seemed laissez-faire about the disappearance of their respective mothers.

"The other part of the problem is that I've had success in the past solving crimes that I was confronted with, and I really felt I could figure the mystery out. However, I forgot about 'embracing your limitations,' which would have kept me from doing too much and burning through my resources. After spending those hours in the OR assisting in a spinal fusion, using my hands to fix a problem, I stepped back from myself for a wake-up call. I'm a surgeon, and I need to use my skills helping folks in a tangible way. I won't totally let go of the information I've gleaned about the disappearances, but I've got to move forward. The issue of these women has to take a back seat. I won't be able to forget about them, though. I couldn't in good conscience allow myself to do that. They will be in my mind, just not in the forefront."

"I don't want you to forget them, Jim Bob. I was quite proud of your efforts to discover what happened to them. But it was taking you over, mind and body, and you were putting yourself in what I thought was a dangerous position. That deputy sheriff husband of your patient worried me, and the Granite Falls cop that stopped us worried me. Above all, I want you safe and healthy."

We fell asleep for a short time and woke up starving. "What do you want to do about dinner?" Mary Louise asked.

"How about I make a pitcher of Tito's vodka martinis, and you have food from Jason's Deli delivered?"

"You have the best ideas, young man."

I stored the freshly made pitcher of martinis in the freezer and took Tip for a walk. The delivery man arrived as I was walking back into the lobby. I paid him, tipped him handsomely, and took the sacks upstairs. I rang the doorbell, holding Tip by the leash in one hand and dinner in the other. Mary Louise answered the door with an odd look on her face. I stepped inside and found a woman unknown to me standing in the kitchen.

"Hello, Dr. Brady, I'm Martha Stevens from the real estate firm."

"Sorry, Jim Bob, for the unexpected visit," Mary Louise said, "but Martha called me after you left. She has an offer on the apartment."

"What? I didn't know we had listed it yet. That was one of the reasons for me to return home, to start that process."

"I gave Martha the listing a month or so ago, when it seemed to me that you were leaning toward moving out to Granite Falls. It's a pocket listing, which means the apartment was not on the MLS but was available to those with inside knowledge about how the system works in our building."

"You'll have to share with me just what the system is."

"Mary Louise, I can answer that for him. Jim, for the past ten years, due to the desirability of the building and its central location to downtown, Greenway Plaza, and the medical center, not a single apartment has been placed on the MLS. All have been private sales, through word of mouth between the residents. Of course, I will still get a healthy commission, but you and Mary Louise will avoid the inconvenience of showings and open houses. I have a full cash offer on your apartment if you two will include the furnishings. My clients fell in love with the place last week. I showed it to them while you were out of town. They are being transferred back to Houston from New York and have dear friends who live in the building who highly recommended your apartment to them."

"Wow. This is sudden, and sort of . . . final. It's a big change.

"Without change, Jim Bob, there would be no butterflies," my dear wife replied.

"Where would we live in Granite Falls?"

"Jim Bob, you left me a message this afternoon that said to list this place, that we're going to the Hill Country. Well, it's done. We can pack our personal items and artwork and be on the road in a few days. If we sign the documents that Martha has prepared, we're done and out of here, just like you said you wanted. I called Chuck while you were on the road driving home and made a verbal offer on the house we liked for the asking price less five percent. You're not changing your mind, are you?"

I hesitated for just a moment. "No, it's just so sudden. But you know me, I'm adaptable."

Mary Louise covered her mouth with her hand, then broke out laughing. "Honey, a lot of wonderful things you are, but that? I'm sorry, but you're a creature of habit, unchanging in your ways. Always have been, and probably always will be. Now sign the papers so we can eat."

Mary Louise called a moving company the next morning, and over the next few days we supervised the packing of our prized possessions. Chuck called us to let us know that our offer was accepted. In my experience, an owner is more apt to accept a lesser amount for a home if the offer is in cash. We would close in thirty days, allowing a title company to charge a startling amount of money to prove that we and we alone would be owners of the Granite Falls house.

Mary Louise had made arrangements with the Hill Country Resort to continue our lease of the apartment on Lake LBJ until we took possession of the new home. I must say, the woman had thought of everything. I could have just sat around and done nothing, which is essentially what I did except for the unnecessary supervision of the packing of my western art.

On the last day in what had been a wonderful residence for a number of years, we finalized the paperwork with Martha and turned over the keys and remotes for the parking garage. She collected the tidy sum of nearly $100,000 for a few phone calls and visits. Nice work if you can get it.

Tip and I stopped and bid adieu to Raj, the doorman and daytime security supervisor. He had the valets pull our cars to the front entry for the last time, and my bride and I drove off to begin a new life.

CHAPTER 21

MURDER

I spent the next month getting ready to return to work. I interviewed secretaries—now called administrative assistants—and nurses. HCMC had a plethora of employees to interview from, and if I didn't find anyone that suited me, Buck Owens said he would bring potential employees in from the outside. I had paperwork to get done for Medicare, Medicaid, and the various insurance plans that were in play at HCMC. I had to complete my application papers to become a staff member, now that I was going to be official. I assisted on quite a few surgeries, which I thoroughly enjoyed, and which would keep me busy and out of trouble. The missing women were still in my mind, but the intensity of my interest was waning. I was doing my best to let the investigators do the investigating, although I knew in my heart that there was no one looking for them.

Mary Louise spent that time upgrading the new house. She hired a crew and replaced the carpets, repainted, repaired electrical outlets and lighting fixtures inside and out, replaced air conditioning and heating equipment, and re-landscaped. We had purchased the house with the furniture, but some was to her liking and some wasn't. What she didn't approve of was given to the crew that worked on the house, and new pieces were brought in from Austin. When she was done, the ten-year-old house felt brand new. We were disappointed but understanding when our long-serving (and long appreciated) housekeeper, Tonita, chose to stay in Houston. But as luck would have it, she happily referred us to her cousin Tonya, who just happened to live in Granite Falls, and in turn Mary Louise happily handed over a spare set of keys.

By some small miracle, the house was completed the day prior to the movers arriving. Once they were there, Mary Louise directed traffic, and a handyman she had hired in advance hung artwork and mirrors and adjusted or replaced art lighting fixtures. It took a day and a half to get it all done, but when it was completed, the place looked spectacular.

We opened a bottle of Veuve Clicquot and had lunch on our expansive patio overlooking Lake LBJ. We toasted each other to a job well done.

My cell phone rang as we finished lunch. It was Lucy Williams, calling to let me know that her daughter and my patient Julie Bates was dead.

"What happened?"

Mary Louise and I were at Lucy's home, trying to give her some comfort in a situation where no comfort was to be found. "She was doing great," Lucy said. "She had been here a month and was up and walking, even taking short walks around the neighborhood with a cane. She seemed happy that Rob had quit coming around. She was off the pain pills, starting to think about going back to work on a part-time basis. And then, this . . ."

She sobbed, Mary Louise wept, and I tried desperately to control my temper.

"It happened yesterday. I went to work as usual, got home about five in the afternoon. Usually she greets me at the front door, but not yesterday. I called her name as I entered, and silence. I walked back to the bedroom she was using and saw that the door was shut. I opened it quietly, thinking she might be napping. and found her. She was nude from the waist down. Her right leg was twisted at an impossible angle, and there was a pillow over her face. I removed it to see if she was breathing, but she was dead. I called 911 and the medics arrived here within ten or fifteen minutes. They confirmed she was gone, then called the Granite Falls police and the medical examiner."

"Why Granite Falls police?"

"I live inside the city limits of Granite Falls."

"What did they say?"

"Not much. They would have to wait for the medical examiner's report, but they said they were suspicious of a rape gone bad."

"I can't imagine a 'good' rape," I said. "She's at the morgue?"

"I would think so, Dr. Brady. Will you go and check on my baby for me?"

That induced another round of sobbing. All I could think of was Rob Bates, the nasty deputy sheriff of Kingsland County.

I offered to take Mary Louise home before I made the trek to the morgue, but she volunteered to stay with Lucy.

The morgue was in a basement in HCMC. I didn't even know there was a basement there, but I located it without much trouble and found a pathologist. His name tag said Dr. Jerry Reed. Were this not a somber visit, I would have pointed out his country-singer name. I introduced myself as a new member of the staff and having been the operating surgeon on Julie Bates's hip and pelvis.

"Have you performed the autopsy on Julie Bates?

"Just completed it. The body's a mess. We don't get many of these in our little neck of the woods, fortunately. Obvious severe bruising in the vaginal vault and exterior in the labial folds as well. Her right femur was fractured below the stem of the prosthesis. It had to have taken some severe force to create that injury. Her cause of death, however, was strangulation. Her hyoid bone was fractured, which is otherwise rare but is commonly seen with strangulation. I have X-rays if you would like to see." He hung them on screens surrounding the autopsy room, much like they do in radiology with living patients' films. Her femur was clearly fractured below the tip of the prosthesis. And her hyoid bone was indeed fractured. He had taken films of her forearm bone, which had been repaired at the same time as I repaired her hip. It was clearly healed.

"Did I mention that there was no sperm or seminal vesicle fluid in the vaginal vault? The killer must have used a condom."

"So no DNA?"

"No. I'll tell you what is weird, though. There wasn't a foreign hair or any sort of skin residue anywhere on her body. The peroneal area had been wiped clean with bleach, so that area was sterilized. But there was nothing around her mouth or on her arms or legs. Whoever it was had to be wearing a full-body covering, like a wet suit, including gloves and a hat or cap of some sort. The body was totally clean. There was nothing to sample for DNA. Not even debris under her fingernails."

"Are you familiar with those cases of the six women who disappeared? Think this could somehow be related?"

"Those women vanished without a trace. Nobody knows what happened to them, except maybe the killer, if there was one. This is a clear case of rape with death by strangulation, and evidence to suggest there was a lot of anger involved in the attack. I personally can't see how they could be related."

By the time I returned to Lucy's house, a close friend of hers had arrived. I told Lucy of my conversation with the pathologist, which created another round of crying. I gave her a hug, and Mary Louise and I went home.

"I have my first patients to see tomorrow, so I'm doing my best to stay focused. I don't know about you, but high on my list of suspects would be the estranged husband, Deputy Sheriff Rob Bates. But, as bad as I want to torture him into telling me the truth about why he killed his wife, I'm going to stay away from him and this case."

We were back on our new patio, staring at the water, drinking Rombauer chardonnay. I had been pleased to discover that the liquor stores in this area carried fine wines and spirits. We may have changed houses, but we didn't have to change our taste in beverages.

Tip was loving the outdoors. There was a stone fence surrounding the backyard, which kept him from chasing critters down the hill and into the lake, but not so high as to obstruct our view. Tip had spent a large part of his life riding up and down in elevators. Running nearly free was a treat for him.

My cell phone rang. It was Buck Owens. "I guess you heard," he said.

"Yes. Mary Louise and I just came from Lucy's. I went over to the morgue and talked to the pathologist. It was a brutal rape and strangulation. Makes me sick."

"Me as well. Lucy works for me, but she's been a good friend for years. It breaks my heart.

"On a subject that we can actually do something about, I hear you're seeing patients tomorrow for the first time. Would you have time to fix a forearm fracture before you begin? Radius and ulna are both broken and need plates. You can have a 7 a.m. operating time."

"Well, sure, that's not my area of expertise, necessarily, but I've repaired a lot of them. No one else around to repair it?"

"Special patient. Be there about 6 a.m., please."

I told Mary Louise about the conversation. "I wonder what a 'special patient' means to Buck Owens," she said.

"No idea. Guess I'll find out in the morning."

CHAPTER 22

SISTER MADS

I arrived at the pre-op area, went into the men's locker room, and changed into scrubs. Either this was a new, modern material that stayed wrinkle-free after washing and drying, or the staff painstakingly ironed the surgical garb. I couldn't imagine the hospital having the staff or the money for that undertaking. I'd have to bring that up with Buck.

There were a few patients in hospital beds, awaiting blood work, IVs, and paperwork completion prior to having surgery. I saw Buck standing beside one of the beds, and I made my way there.

"I'd like you to meet Madeline O'Rourke, Jim," he said. "We call her Sister Mads."

"Morning," I said, to him, the nurse also standing at the bedside, and the patient. She was a tiny woman with white hair cut very short, and she couldn't have been much over five feet tall. She had to weigh under a hundred pounds and appeared to be in her early seventies, but she had this radiant glow to her wrinkled face. I shook her hand. She grabbed mine in both of hers, in spite of the splint on her left wrist, and kissed the top of my fingers. That was a first for me.

"You're doing the Lord's work this morning, young man. You're putting an old woman back together so she can continue fighting the good fight. I'm not down for the count, yet. I've got lots of fight left in me. So you do your very best, and I'll continue to spread the joy."

All I could think of to say was "Yes, ma'am."

After the nursing assistants wheeled her off toward the operating room, I asked Buck about Sister Mads.

"She was a nun for many years, working out of a convent in Austin. She became interested in helping battered and abused women and organized a shelter at the convent. Over time, the shelter became very well known. Most shelters such as this have to operate in the dark out of necessity, in order to protect the women who have found their way there. In time, some of the women that came needed a pregnancy terminated, and word got back to the archdiocese that Sister Mads was arranging or making referrals for that procedure, and the archbishop put his foot down, backed by the Catholic Church hierarchy. The shelter could stay open, and the Church would continue to fund it, but there would be NO abortions performed on the women that the Church was assisting.

"Sister Mads insisted on providing a 'full service' shelter and refused to back down. As a result, the Church threw her out for failure to uphold her vows. Mads had seen this coming and contacted me and a number of other benefactors to see if they would be willing to assist in privatizing her shelter. I agreed, as did many other supporters in the Austin area."

"How did you get involved with her initially?" I asked.

"I had a niece that found herself in dire straits some years ago, and I contacted several friends and agencies to get her help. I was referred to Mads's convent; Our Lady of the Lake, it was called. She and I became great friends over the years. She got my niece to a better place and has helped hundreds, maybe thousands to regain their lives away from abusive husbands.

"So Mads left the convent, moved into her own facility with the help of many friends, and went into a somewhat different line of work. She now runs an organization that not only helps battered and abused women get away from their abusers, but provides educational opportunities, legal advice, temporary housing, medical care, even relocation services. It's called Mourning Doves," he said.

My mouth dropped open. "Mourning Doves? My son J .J. came across that name when he was doing some research for me into the backgrounds of the women that disappeared. That's the organization that all six women sent money to every month."

"That is correct. The facility depends on donations from many friends such as me, plus grants from the local, state, and federal government. Women who have been through the facility, once back on their feet, are also asked to contribute money to sustain Sister Mads's services. Sort of a payback for previous help, but also a pay-it-forward concept.

"With all that said, I'd like to meet you and Mary Louise for dinner and discuss Mourning Doves at length."

The surgery on Sister Mads went well. I was able to plate both fractures and restore alignment. I splinted the forearm, dictated my operative report, and went to the waiting room to talk to family members that might be present. There was no one to speak to, so I returned to the locker I had been assigned, changed back into street clothes, and walked down to the first floor, then over to the clinic building for my first day of office patients. With a few minutes to spare, I wandered the clinic building space. There was a pharmacy and a cafeteria on the first level, with examination rooms and doctor's offices on the second and third floors. I estimated there was at least 50,000 square feet per floor, maybe more. It wasn't as massive a space as the hospital side, but there was plenty of room for expansion.

The second floor was composed primarily of a large central waiting room, with exam rooms constructed in a pie-shaped fashion behind doors that led from the waiting area into the rear of the space. Each sector had a small nursing station/dictation area, with four or five exam rooms in close proximity. There were seven of these clustered in a semicircular fashion, with radiology at one end and a cast room at the other. The cast room had six tables for applying casts and splints to the injured.

I took the stairs up to the third floor and found that to be the location of the physicians' private offices, as well as the administration department. I wandered the area and found an office door with my name on it. The door was unlocked. I entered the small space, about ten by twelve, with a nice window and a view of the Hill Country. I don't know when she'd had time, but Mary Louise had dropped off books, mementos, and framed diplomas, and had decorated the office in a grand style.

I sat in my reclining office chair and thought about Mourning Doves. The missing women had made use of Mads's facility at some point in their lives, based on their contributions, helping to pay it forward, as Buck put it. Did this mean they had recovered their lives, only to be struck down by an assailant after surviving past horrors of abuse? I just didn't get it. There had to be more to the story. I would arrange for Mary Louise and I to sit down at dinner and discuss the organization with Buck, as he suggested.

I saw ten patients that first day in the new office. Shelly Wood had been assigned to be my nurse because I had been unable to choose one from the nursing pool. She had been working at HCMC since it opened five years prior. Shelly had elected to "float" in the nursing pool, rather than accept an assignment to a particular physician. I liked her immediately. She was born in East Texas and educated in Houston, with degrees in nursing and English. She was a voracious reader and fond of communicating with quotes from her favorite authors. Shelly was short and thin, with black hair going to prematurely gray. She favored large designer glasses rather than contacts.

I was used to seeing a vast number of patients on a clinic day, so having only ten to see gave me the opportunity to take my time and get to know folks. Four of the patients had undergone previous hip replacement, and symptoms had recurred. X-rays were suggestive of loosening, and Shelly scheduled MRI scans to confirm. Two patients had hip arthritis, had already been to radiology, had arthritis confirmed by X-rays and scans, and scheduled replacement. Two patients had early arthritic symptoms, confirmed by X-ray, but were not severe enough to warrant surgery.

One patient, a young teenage football player, had sustained a dislocated hip in a game three months prior. He wanted to return to athletics but needed clearance from a physician. His X-rays did not show evidence of avascular necrosis of the femoral head . . . yet. Oftentimes, when the hip is traumatically dislocated, the blood supply is disrupted and the head of the femur dies and turns to chalk, and severe arthritis ensues. There were no signs on plain films, but I suggested scans to see the hip in greater detail before I made that decision. He was disappointed, but his mother was relieved.

The last patient was a middle-aged female who had made an appointment for follow-up on a fractured humerus, the upper arm bone. She allegedly broke it during a fall down the stairs in her home, carrying a tray on which she had delivered food to her aging mother, who was living with her. X-rays confirmed the fracture—fractures, actually, since there was one main spiral fracture and two other small ones adjacent to the large one. I didn't see any healing yet, but it had only been a week. There was a great deal of bruising and swelling in the arm. She was in a fabricated sling and was using a splint at night to help her sleep. The man with her identified himself as her husband and was most interested to know when his wife could return to her normal "chores" like cooking and cleaning. I told him at least three months, and that did not make him happy. His attitude was not one of caring and concern. He muttered something about "sending the old lady to a nursing home." I excused myself and let Shelly schedule a follow-up appointment for two weeks and deal with trying to get them home health services. If there was a silver lining for the patient, it was that the fracture was in her left arm, and she was right-handed.

I dictated my office-visit findings into a voice-activated computer, which stored the data into the electronic medical records system. I could print anything I needed in the records system, but the goal was to "go paperless." Medical records could be accessed at any location with a compatible system. HCMC was a branch of a huge hospital system headquartered in Dallas, so if a patient sought medical care anywhere in the system, previous medical records could be retrieved through the computer hard drive almost instantly. Whether this system was compatible with other hospital computer systems was above my pay grade.

We finished seeing patients around 2 p.m. I thanked Shelly for a good first day and told her that I would like to resume my old schedule of seeing patients Tuesday and Thursday and performing surgery on Monday and Wednesday. And that absent emergencies, I would attend to the ills and wants of my golf game on Friday, Saturday, and Sunday.

I walked over to the hospital and checked on Sister Mads. She was wide awake and feisty as hell.

"I need to get back to work, Doctor. May I leave today?"

"No ma'am, you need to stay overnight so the nursing staff can check the circulation in your fingers. If you're all right in the morning, I'll take off that splint and put you in a hard cast."

"For how long?"

"Two weeks. Then we'll visit in the clinic, get an X-ray, and hopefully put you in a removable splint so you can take a shower."

"I see. Well, you have to dance with who 'brung' you, as the old saying goes, so I'm at your mercy. Have you discussed Mourning Doves yet with Buck?"

"Not yet. Mary Louise—my wife—and I are going to have dinner with Buck and broach that subject. He seemed mysterious about it."

"Damn right. What we do there is private, and the fewer wrong people that know about it, the better."

"The wrong people?"

"He'll tell you all about it. Now go help some sick people, Doctor. I'm going to be fine."

"By the way, you didn't mention how you broke your arm."

"That's right, I didn't. Doing battle, fighting the good fight, that's how."

I called Mary Louise from the car to check on our social schedule, which she said was nonexistent, so we could have dinner with Buck anytime, including tonight.

I then called Buck and told him we were available. He invited us to his home, rather than a restaurant, for privacy reasons, he said.

CHAPTER 23

MOURNING DOVES

Buck lived in a beautiful home on the water in a small gated community with only four houses. He asked us to come over at four in the afternoon so that we could enjoy a boat ride at sunset. He had a spectacular view across Lake LBJ, with two boat docks adjacent to his large patio. He loaded a couple of bottles of wine and some snacks into what I would call a speedboat, and we three took off across the lake, slowly building up speed after we passed through the "No Wake" zone.

Once he reached cruising speed, talking was difficult. So, Mary Louise and I sipped our wine and munched on small smoked-salmon bites on crackers with cream cheese and capers. Once we were out in the middle of the lake, Buck slowed the boat down and steered it off to the east side of the lake and into a cove. There was a large home in the center of the cove, with vacant land on either side. Parked in the dock were two Jet Skis, a speed boat, and a large Duffy electric cruising boat.

"My wife Alicia died twelve years ago of breast cancer. She had been with me since medical school, so it was a great loss to me. I think I mentioned that I started out in family practice, then got lucky in the oil business with some old friends and became a wealthy man. I worked in the oil fields for a while but got bored with it. I wanted to be in some area of medicine but just didn't want the day-to-day grind. Alicia had this idea that we should build a state-of-the-art hospital, along with satellite clinics for patients' convenience. She and I had talked about it for years. Once she died, I was paralyzed for a year, couldn't really do anything. Then, I woke up one morning and decided the hospital would be a great project in her honor.

"I gathered together some of my wealthy friends, here and in the Austin area, and put together a plan. We all put in money to finance construction, then partnered with a large hospital/clinic conglomerate out of Dallas, got our certificate of need from the State of Texas, and went to work. It took two years to build the hospital and clinic buildings and another year to get it staffed. We were not guaranteed any patients, of course, so we worked on the concept from the movie *Field of Dreams:* if you build it, they will come. And they did. We've been up and running for seven years. We pay top dollar for nursing and ancillary staff. The docs all get a generous salary, and the hospital covers their overhead costs, malpractice insurance, and continuing-medical-education expenses, along with a generous vacation package. The dream Alicia and I had years ago had come to fruition. I enjoyed myself immensely for a while, and then got bored again.

"About that time, Madeline O'Rourke got in touch with me. We had known each other for years as a result of my niece's problems with her ex. Sister Mads was being thrown out of the convent for stepping over the boundaries of the Church one too many times. She wanted to continue her work but needed to set up her own facility, and she wanted to know if I could help. So, I went back to my friends and investors, gave them a rundown on the kind of work she was doing, and once again, they opened up their respective wallets. And there it is. Mourning Doves," he said, and pointed to the home in the center of the cove.

"It's been open for four years now. Mads has helped hundreds of women who had been battered or abused in some way to recover their lives. She has strict parameters for admittance, however. She can handle twenty women at any one time. She doesn't take kids. Alcohol and drugs are strictly forbidden. If a resident is caught using, or drunk, they are out immediately. The stay is two months. She provides educational counseling, legal services, even relocation assistance when the situation dictates. There is a long waiting list to get in. Her goal is to change a woman's life, make her self-sufficient, and teach her to avoid putting herself back in the same situation that brought her to Mourning Doves in the first place. Mads has had dramatic success with her program."

Mary Louise spoke up. "Buck, I worked at the women's center in Houston, on the hotline. It seems to me that the shelters there for the most part involved very transient people. A night or two stay, at the most. Many were emergency rescues, brought in by a friend or family member, sometimes with children in tow. Then they would move on. I always wondered what happened to them after only a day or two. That never seemed long enough to change their lives or get themselves out of the dangerous situation they found themselves in."

"Mary Louise, that's the beauty of Mads's program. She is in the business of changing the parameters of her residents' lives. Most centers can only put a Band-Aid on the problem. She intends to cure the problem in the clients she accepts. She knows she can't fix everybody. She's been down that road before at the convent."

"I don't see how she can possibly cure the problem if there is no treatment for the abuser," responded Mary Louise.

"Her philosophy is that you can't cure the abuser. You can cure the acceptance of abuse as a way of life and change the woman's dynamic by putting her in a different situation with a different frame of mind. That's why the two-month stay. You can't fix a situation in one or two days."

Buck gassed the boat out of idle and steered us back into the center of the Lake LBJ. Once idle, we clinked our glasses and watched the sun melt into a fiery pool and disappear.

Back at Buck's home, we were treated to a catered dinner of Caesar salad, pork tenderloin, fresh vegetables, and peach pie with ice cream. Over a snifter of brandy on his deck, he told us he would like us to get involved with Mourning Doves.

"How?" asked Mary Louise.

"Financially, of course. It takes a lot of money to run the . . . charity, if you will. For you, my dear, I would appreciate you volunteering at the center, maybe once a week. We try and keep salaries to a minimum. Mads has the women residing there provide housekeeping services and food preparation. They also do the landscaping and keep the boats and dock clean. She has to bring in outside staff for mechanical and electrical repairs and maintenance but tries to keep that to a minimum. Shopping would have been an issue—we try and keep our residents on campus—so we use the delivery services, via boat, of one specified and trusted HEB employee.

"For your husband here, he would have more of a hands-on role. For example, he fixed Mads's forearm fracture this morning. From time to time, he would participate in medical care and other surgeries as needed. There won't be any remuneration for those services, Jim Bob. You would be doing this out of the goodness of your heart."

"I'm curious if this meeting tonight has something to do with my looking into the disappearances of those six women."

"Yes. I received several calls from local bankers, who reported that a hacker got into their records, and coincidentally, all the accounts accessed had auto-pay payments to Mourning Doves. I also received calls from Robert Allen, Hilary's son, and Deborah Smith, Katie Smith's daughter. I believe Robert actually met with you, and Deborah spoke to you on the phone. They were both worried about you continuing to dig into their mothers' lives and discover facts that might disrupt all of our planning and work. I called the other four kids of our disappeared mothers and told them not to return your phone call.

"I was most worried you might somehow inadvertently alert the husbands of the missing women as to the particulars of their wives' disappearances. I don't think you knew enough to do that yet, but you were digging into confidential information and I didn't know how far you would get. Those of us who are involved in this business felt you were getting close to discovering our secret, so I thought it best to bring you two on board."

I glanced at Mary Louise. "On board what?"

"Mourning Doves. Those six women? They're ours. We made them disappear."

CHAPTER 24

SECRETS AND LIES

After dropping that bombshell news on us, Buck thought we had heard enough for one evening, and said that we would get together soon and he would then answer any questions we might have. Mary Louise and I kept staring at each other on the way home. How in the world could a conspiracy of that magnitude be kept secret? Mourning Doves would have to be the epicenter of the ruse, but many other individuals would have to be kept in the loop to ensure a successful "disappearance" of these women. Was family in the know? Bankers? Nurses at the hospital? The list of potential co-conspirators seemed endless. And what about law enforcement? Could police officers and sheriff deputies be involved? I couldn't imagine that, since the more people involved, the bigger the task to keep the scheme under wraps.

And why were those women chosen to vanish? Had they experienced the worst abuse? Or were they more self-sufficient than others, or had family money and could afford to disappear? And what were the mechanics of the vanishing? What about automobiles, credit cards, and cash requirements? How could someone simply be working, living with someone, participating in a life one day, albeit an abusive one, and the next day be completely gone and never heard from again?

When we got home, we poured ourselves a roadie and took Tip out for a walk. We left our little enclave and walked down the entry street, asked each other a myriad of questions, and returned thirty minutes later without a single answer. Neither of us could get a handle on exactly how these disappearances could happen. We went to bed still asking questions, but no answers were forthcoming.

I woke up in the middle of the night and got up and drank some Gatorade. I figured I could use the potassium. The thought had occurred to me that both Robert Allen and Deborah Smith were involved in their respective mother's disappearance. They were both pretty cagey about the mystery, even seeming unconcerned about the vanishing. I should have known then that something fishy was going on. I even remembered telling Mary Louise they seemed more worried about the cities they were living in than about their mothers.

And what did it actually mean when Buck said he had to "bring us on board"? What were we getting ourselves involved in? We had just purchased a home, I had my first clinic in the new location, and to top that off we're involved in the guise of kidnapping women trying to get away from bad husbands?

And where did the murder of Julie Bates fit in? Was this related to the disappearances? And when was the funeral? We shouldn't miss that, for Lucy's sake.

I went back to bed and tossed and turned for a while until I finally slept an exhausted and fitful sleep.

Next morning, I went to the hospital to see Buck. Lucy was working; how, I don't know.

She stood, walked around her desk, and hugged me.

"I can't believe you're here after what you been through, Lucy. Shouldn't you take a few days off?"

"That what Dr. Owens said, but when I'm not here, all I think about is Lucy, and how horrible the end of her life had to be. At least if I'm working, my mind can dwell on other issues."

"Is he in today?"

"Yes, but he's in a meeting. I do want to tell you something, though. I met with Dr. Owens this morning, and he told me that you had been investigating the missing women on your own. He ended up deciding to tell you and your wife about Mourning Doves, since he felt you were the kind of people who would be able to get involved and keep all you learned confidential. At any rate, he gave me permission to tell you about Lucy. As you know, over the past year, a woman went missing every two months."

"Yes. I remember that someone from law enforcement called in a profiler from the FBI to study the cases. And her conclusion was that if it were a serial rapist or kidnapper, another woman would go missing in November. But it didn't happen. And since there was no clue whatsoever as to what happened to the women, the investigation was basically dropped. That was one of the reasons I started looking for answers. I didn't want the women who disappeared to not have a voice."

"And we all appreciate that, Dr. Brady. But what I wanted you to know was that before the so-called car accident, Julie was supposed to be the November, or seventh, disappearance. She was all ready and primed, and all the arrangements had been made. She was due to leave the next day, following her shift in radiology. Twenty-four hours to freedom, then hit by a car. And now she's dead."

I held her while she sobbed.

Once Lucy gathered herself together, she told me the funeral was to be day after tomorrow, and she hoped that Mary Louise and I could attend. I assured her we would be there.

I walked over to the clinic building and had breakfast in the cafeteria on the first floor. I was finishing my ham and eggs when the cell phone buzzed. Lucy said Dr. Owens was back in his office and wanted me to stop by before I left.

I went upstairs to my new office and checked for mail and any documents I needed to sign. By some miracle, my desk was clean. Nurse Shelly Wood wasn't around, so I left for the hospital.

I went up to the third floor and saw Sister Mads. Her circulation was excellent, so the nurses wheeled her over to the cast room and I assisted the cast technician in the application of a relatively waterproof plastic cast. It came with a rubber cast cover just in case water leaked around the edges.

"I'll sign your discharge papers. Do you have a ride home?"

"Of course, Dr. Brady. I'll see you in a couple of weeks. And I'm glad to hear you're on board. Buck told me."

"Well, I don't know what it entails yet, but I'm sure I'll find out soon enough."

"Yes you will, dearie, yes you will." She hugged me around the neck and kissed me on the cheek.

Back in Buck's office, he handed me a thick file folder.

"For your and Mary Louise's eyes only. That's all confidential stuff. Keep it in a safe place. These are copies of the originals, but don't make more copies. Do not allow this information to get out of your hands."

"I have many questions, Buck."

"I'm sure you do. After you've read through all the material, we'll meet and I'll answer any questions you and Mary Louise might have."

"But—"

"Please. Read the material, then we'll talk again."

I was reeling from too much information already when Lucy told me that Julie was to be the seventh disappearance. I didn't get that at all. There was an orchestrated pattern of a woman vanishing every other month, and her daughter was to be the latest. Maybe these seven women weren't high profile in a big-city sort of way, but they all were known in the communities around Lake LBJ, had jobs, and most had children, although grown for the most part. What was the logic in that? It's not like no one would miss them. I mean, Hilary Allen was a vice president at a bank; she leaves work for the day and voluntarily disappears? What about her clients? I needed to know what about their lives was so terrible that these women risked everything to simply vanish into thin air? I hoped these papers I held in my hands would give me the explanations that I needed.

When I arrived at my car, I noticed a sheriff's department vehicle close by. I didn't see anyone in the driver's seat, so I assumed they perhaps were a patient at the clinic. Wrong.

"Whatcha got there, Doc?" said Rob Bates, deputy sheriff of Kingsland County and husband of the deceased Julie Bates.

"Hospital charts and medical records of patients I'm either seeing or going to see tomorrow." I lied as best I could. "I am sorry for your loss."

He heaved a sigh. "Well, we hadn't been together in a while, so it's not like we were playing husband and wife, if you get my drift. When I catch the guy that did her in . . . well, let's just say that we won't have to worry about jail time."

And here I was thinking he was the guilty party, and maybe he was, but he sounded like he was going to put the blame on someone other than himself. And I'll bet he could find plenty of criminals to frame for the murder if need be.

"I have to run. Nice to see you," I lied again, and after I literally threw the documents into the passenger seat, I offered him a handshake.

"I appreciate the condolences. Julie and I could have had a good life together, were it not for that bitch mother of hers. Always sticking her nose in our business. 'Are you limping?' 'Is that a bruise on your cheek?' 'What's wrong with your arm?' Comments like that. Julie was a klutz with a capital K. Always tripping and falling, always had some of injury or another. Anyway, you take care, Doc. Keep a lookout for the bad guys. Never know when they'll sneak up on you." He tipped his Stetson, sidled over to his car, and left the parking lot.

CHAPTER 25

SUSAN BEESON

I called Mary Louise to tell her I was on my way home and asked what she wanted to do about lunch. She said she was making lunch at home, and that she had a surprise for me. I told her I couldn't handle any more surprises. She laughed and said she would see me soon.

When I walked into the great room, I put the load of paper down on the kitchen bar—and almost ran into the Houston chief of police, Susan Beeson. We had been friends for years and had initially met when she was a detective with HPD. I would always be in her debt for saving Mary Louise and I from a certain death by an evil and deranged nurse from Louisiana.

Susan was still in her "uniform," which was black slacks, white collared dress shirt, black blazer, and what I always referred to as her comfortable shoes: black brogans. The job of chief of police of the nation's fourth-largest city had aged her. Her hair was going gray, and I noted frown lines on her forehead and smile lines on her cheeks, although probably not from smiling.

We hugged. That would be three for the day.

"What in the world are you doing here?" I asked.

"Job interview. Mary Louise and I have been talking, and she has told me repeatedly how wonderful this place is. I received a call three months ago about a position in Austin with the FBI, so I thought, why not come and get a first-hand look."

"The FBI? I was sure you would keep the police chief job until you were ready to retire."

"Jim, everything changes, and there are no answers."

"Wow. I need to remember that one. That's a credo to live by."

"The position that I interviewed for is the ASAC—Assistant Special Agent in Charge, which would cover the area from Austin west, essentially the western half of Texas. Both San Antonio and Dallas have that position as well, so there would be some overlap in jurisdiction. I thought it would be interesting and a nice change of pace. I'm more of a politician these days, trying to keep the various factions in the city from killing each other. I think it would be challenging to be an investigator again. That's what I did when I was a detective, back in the day."

"How's your dad?" I asked.

"More crochety than ever. Still complains about the hip you replaced years ago. You know, my son is in middle school, if you can fathom that."

"How time flies. Listen, is there a profiler working out of the Austin office?"

"Yes, but she's gone. She somehow botched a case involving some missing women from out here in the Lakes area and was transferred to Anchorage. I don't know all the details."

Mary Louise looked at me, chuckled, and shook her head.

"Susan, have I got a story for you."

We had a delicious lunch of Caesar salad with anchovies, grilled mahi-mahi, and a broccolini and cauliflower casserole. I treated us to a cold bottle of pinot grigio.

The sun was out and the temperature was mild, so we moved out to the patio-deck-terrace for coffee and conversation.

"Let me explain my involvement with the mystery of the vanishing women. I was eating lunch on the north side of the lake at the Crazy Gals Cafe, and saw the *Highlander,* a local newspaper servicing the Lakes area. There was an article about these six women who had disappeared, starting in November last year and going through September of this year. I searched the internet and found an article written by a graduate student in journalism at UT. She went into some depth about each of the missing women and mentioned that an FBI profiler had been called in by law enforcement and had studied the cases. Her conclusion was there was no evidence to profile. All leads were dead ends. She suggested that if there was a pattern, someone would have to vanish in November, which did not happen, at least as far as anyone knows. Someone could have disappeared in November, but given the previous parameters, nothing fit the pattern. So, the investigation essentially dried up."

"That sounds like the case I heard about," Susan replied. "The husband of one of the women made a stink about the incompetence of local law enforcement as well as the FBI during an interview with a news commentator. And nothing riles the feds up more than a complaint about one of their own from a taxpayer."

"Do you know which husband made the complaint?"

"No, but I could find out if I take the job. I think Gene likes the idea, and our son, well, he'll have to enroll in a new school. But he's the gregarious type and loves golf and boating, so he's a shoo-in to okay the move."

"I haven't been through all these records yet, but I find it hard to believe what I'm told happened. The planning and execution, flawless. But I have many questions, so I'd rather not say more until I glean what I can from all this paperwork. Do you want to get involved, Susan? Mary Louise and I are committed, but to exactly what, we're not quite sure."

"Your dear wife invited me to stay the night, so I'm game. I don't have to be back in Houston until tomorrow noon. I would like to ask you one thing before we begin, and that's if these women came from the same town."

"Susan, this area is unique. You can be driving along a street and you're in Horseshoe Bay. Next thing you know, you're in Cottonwood Shores. Then it changes to Granite Falls, then Marble Falls. Depending on your route, you could end up in Burnet, or Granite Shoals, or Kingsland. And you're always in a small city, with businesses, churches, fast-food establishments. There seems to be a central Walmart, and a gigantic H-E-B that services the other small towns. These places are contiguous, and I imagine they have their own city services and local governments and police departments. But you can't tell it by driving around, except to see a sign declaring this to be the city limits of whichever town you happen to be in at the moment. These women were all from the Highland Lakes area, which is a conglomerate of all these small towns.

"I've compiled information on these women from two sources. One is from the comprehensive article by the UT journalism grad student, and the other is from our son, J. J., who is still in the private investigation business, as you probably know. There is a large dossier on each woman that Dr. Buck Owens gave me this morning. These records I have not reviewed."

"Who is Buck Owens?" Susan asked.

"President and CEO of HCMC, and is somehow involved in these women and their disappearances. Also, there is a former nun, Sister Mads she's called, who is involved through an organization called Mourning Doves."

"I've heard of Mourning Doves. High-end women's shelter, very private."

I nodded. "There are seven folders here. I'll take three and you each take two, and we'll—"

"Why seven if there were six women who vanished?" Susan asked.

"I'll get to that later. I don't know what's in these folders as far as private information about each woman. There is an undercurrent of abuse associated with the disappearances, so I can't tell you how graphic this stuff might be. Let's read, and summarize, then talk about each. I think it will help me to see this from your perspectives, and also to re-familiarize myself with data I might have forgotten.

"I'll take Julie Bates"—Mary Louise's eyes widened in recognition—"Hilary Allen, and Katie Smith. Mary Louise, you take Margaret Harris and Carla Robinson. Susan, you take Karen Statton and Jorja Watson, if that's all right with the two of you."

We three read in silence for a while. Then, I heard some deep breaths and sighs from my co-readers, and soon I found myself mumbling obscenities about the details of these women's lives. My God, what has the world come to, I thought. I noticed copies of several legal documents—affidavits, police reports, and restraining orders—in the back of each of the three files I was reviewing. I was starting to get a picture of chronic abuse with enmity between the victims, law enforcement, and legal counsel. I had poked a hornet's nest by involving myself in these women's problems. And now I had involved my wife and her best friend. Good going, Brady.

CHAPTER 26

THE REAL STORY

"I'd like both of you to take notes and I'll do the same, so we can review all this info later.

"Let me start with Katie Smith. She disappeared January 15, at age fifty-two. She worked as an event planner at Hill Country Resort and vanished after a function that ended around eight thirty in the evening. Her husband is a local dentist. She has two grown children, one of whom—by the name of Deborah—I spoke to on the phone. She acted as though she had no clue about the vanishing of her mother. Her brother did not return my call. Katie had six visits to the HCMC emergency room over a three-year period. Her husband brought her in for all her visits except the last one, when her sister brought her in. She was treated for a neck sprain, a fractured ankle which required surgery, two shoulder dislocations, a broken nose, and lastly a D&C, at which time it was discovered she was eight weeks pregnant. She gave logical explanations for all these injuries and problems to the ER staff, and no suspicions were noted in the file on any of these visits.

"However, there are numerous legal documents in here, including affidavits signed by the husband, in which he admits to causing all the injures. The neck sprain was caused when she 'smarted off,' and he grabbed her around the neck and threw her down the stairs. The broken ankle occurred after he kicked her with a boot on while holding her body to keep her from running away. The shoulder dislocations came from pulling her arm and swinging her into an interior wall. The broken nose? He punched her in the face when she said she hated him. And lastly, the D&C. He had raped her two months prior in a fit of rage, discovered a home pregnancy test from the bathroom waste can that confirmed she was pregnant, and promptly punched her in the stomach until she started to bleed vaginally.

"Looking at these documents, it appears that some sort of agreement was reached between her lawyers and her husband and his lawyers. He would admit to causing the injuries, in exchange for her not pressing charges. She would be able to disappear from sight and he would not attempt to pursue her. If he did, the affidavits would be handed to the local prosecutor, charges would be filed, and he would, like in Monopoly, go directly to jail.

"Next, Hilary Allen. She disappeared at age forty-six on September 17. She was an executive with Lake Savings and Trust and wasn't seen again after a business lunch at Forno's. Her husband is a litigation attorney in Austin. I spoke to one of her children, Robert, who is a teller at her bank. His main concern was moving back to Austin, not discovering what happened to his mother. She has two other children, one a senior in college and one in law school. They did not return my phone calls.

"Hilary made three visits to the ER, the first due to a fractured lumbar process, and the next two because of persistent pain. Her sister brought her to the ER all three times. She attributed the injury to a fall, but in an affidavit, again signed by the husband, he admitted to throwing her on the floor and jumping onto her lower back repeatedly in a fit of rage. I see the same sort of documents in the file as in Katie's. She won't press charges unless he seeks her out. That seems to be a pattern so far."

"Mary Louise, why don't you go next."

"Margaret Harris, age thirty-seven, was the first; she disappeared November 12, over a year ago. She was a dispatcher with Big Tex Trucking Company and was not seen again after leaving work in the early evening. Her husband is a detective with the Granite Falls Police Department. She had no children. She made two visits to the ER, the first for a concussion she sustained after a fall at home, the second for a fractured wrist allegedly caused by breaking up a dog fight. Her husband took her to the ER both trips. I have similar affidavits in the files, where the husband admits to causing her injuries. The concussion came from him hitting her in the back of the head with a police baton when she refused to have sex with him because she was on her period. The wrist fracture occurred when he bent her wrist backward until it broke because she had worked late and dinner wasn't on the table when he got home.

"Like your two cases, no charges will be filed as long as he gives her a wide berth, wherever she might be."

"Carla Robinson, age forty-four, disappeared March 9. She was a nurse at HCMC on the three-to-eleven shift and vanished after leaving work. Her husband is a long-haul trucker with Big Tex Trucking. She has a daughter who is a senior at Texas State. She made two trips to the ER, the first for a punctured lung due to a fractured rib that occurred when she fell off a ladder. The other was for a lengthy laceration on the sole of her foot that allegedly occurred while chasing her dog through a nearby vacant lot. Her mother brought her in on both occasions. The affidavit states that her husband admitted to kicking her repeatedly in the chest until he felt her ribs break because he suspected her of having an affair while he was on the road. The laceration he made with a Bowie knife, again due to a suspected affair. She denied having an affair repeatedly, in spite of the torture. The file includes similar affidavits to the others you've discussed."

"Susan, you have the floor."

"Karen Statton, age forty-eight, disappeared May 13. She worked as an ICU nurse at HCMC on the day shift, seven in the morning to three in the afternoon. She didn't show up for her weekly canasta game at five in the afternoon. Her husband is an engineer at the Ferguson power plant. She has one son, a senior in medical school in Houston. She had two ER visits, the first for a strep throat, the second for a dislocated patella, or kneecap, that she said occurred spontaneously. Her husband brought her to the ER on both occasions.

"There is an affidavit in the file, but the dates of abusive activity don't correspond to the ER visit dates I noted in the records. There are seven additional dates over the last two years where she made trips to the ER, accompanied by her mother. These visits involved requests for pain medication for various problems, such as back pain, vague abdominal pain, migraine headaches, and radiating leg pain. I don't know why the dates of ER visits don't correspond to the dates of abuse. I guess all these women could have had other ER visits that we don't have documented. At any rate, in the affidavit, the husband admits to causing the problems she complained about to the ER staff with various punches, slaps, shoves, and kicks. Although he admits to the abuse, he stated that his wife was a drug addict, sort of like Nurse Jackie from the television show, and he couldn't stand to be around her because of her drug-seeking behavior.

"Next is Jorja Watson, age thirty-nine, disappeared July 11. She and her husband owned Bay Country Realty—maybe he still does. She vanished around eleven in the morning after a property showing, failing to show up for her next appointment. She has no children. She had one ER visit, presenting with a Q-tip stuck in her ear. Her eardrum was punctured. In the affidavit, the husband admitted to walking into the bathroom while she was sitting in a makeup chair cleaning her ears, when he slapped her hand as hard as he could against the side of her head, embedding the Q-tip. His reason for that incident was to teach her a lesson about what he called her slacker-like behavior toward selling real estate."

"I don't know about you two, but I feel the need to take a shower," I said.

They both agreed. Instead, we made Tito's vodka dirty martinis.

While sipping the needed alcohol relief from the sagas of these abused women, I reported my summary of the file and the story on Julie Bates, the "November woman" whose escape failed to happen. I went through the surgery to repair her hip, pelvis, and forearm fracture, the post-op recovery, her time on the rehab unit, and her eventual rape and murder after she returned to her mother's house.

"Are you telling me that there was not a shred of evidence on the body? No hairs, no fluids, nothing that would provide material for DNA testing?"

"That's right, Susan. The pathologist presumed the attacker used a condom and had on some type of total body covering, like a wetsuit. Also, the lower abdomen and peroneal area was wiped down with bleach to remove any trace evidence in the area. He thought it might be the work of a professional."

"I would agree, Jim. I've seen many off these kinds of cases over my years in law enforcement, and this sounds like a job done by a professional, or at least a very knowledgeable perp."

"Did I mention her husband is a deputy sheriff in Kingsland County?"

"Yes, you did."

"And did I mention he has accosted me three times, twice after Julie's surgery, and once after her murder?"

"Yes, you did."

"What do you make of that?"

"I don't know, Jim."

"You're FBI."

"No, I'm the Houston police chief."

"Well, you're about to be FBI. You need to figure this out. Would you have jurisdiction in this and the other cases we've discussed?"

"Yes, the FBI has jurisdiction over violent offenses like assault, kidnapping, and homicide."

"Well, Susan, the way I see it, these cases involve a lot of assaults. And as far as anyone knows, these women were all kidnapped. And it's pretty clear that Julie Bates was murdered. It's the perfect FBI case, even if it turns out that the missing women weren't really kidnapped but simply escaped from a life of misery and pain.

"By the way, you'll note I didn't mention an agreement in Julie's file. I wouldn't be surprised if they didn't even broach the subject with the deputy. He doesn't seem the type to be moved, let alone intimidated, by an attorney's presentation of that proposal."

"I wonder if someone involved with these cases has kept records of the whereabouts of the six women, if in fact they were runaways, as Buck implied to you," Mary Louise pondered aloud. "Wouldn't you think Buck or Sister Mads would have a way to get in touch with them? What if one of their children needed them, or a mother or sister was ill or injured? I can see disappearing from years of abuse, and hiding from your past, but how in the world does a woman like that stay hidden? Surely their new identities and locations wouldn't be known to everyone. The list of people who could contact each of these women would have to very short."

"You have a very good point, Mary Louise," I replied. "The more people that know the whereabouts of someone hiding increases the chance of them being found. If you look at the six men who have signed affidavits in these files, they certainly have a lot to lose if this material became public knowledge—especially their freedom. You have a police detective, a lawyer, an engineer, a truck driver, a real estate broker, and a dentist. All men with the means to pay for information regarding their missing spouses. But men who would certainly go to jail if their spousal abuse came to light.

"Buck wants to have another conversation with us. We should discuss these issues with him, maybe include Sister Mads in the meeting to get her perspective as well. As you said, it's one thing to help women disappear; it's a whole different project to keep them hidden."

CHAPTER 27

FUNERAL

Mary Louise had a safe installed in the master bedroom closet the next morning. It was one of those 500-pound jobs, so heavy that even if a burglar somehow had the luck and wherewithal to get into the house and locate the safe, it would be impossible to carry it out. She used the excuse of wanting to keep her jewelry safe, but she and I both had the unspoken agreement that the documents we had reviewed were toxic as hell and needed to be kept hidden at all costs. There was a set of originals somewhere, probably with the new identities of the missing women, and more than likely under Buck's purview. But one never knows, does one, so we felt it important to keep our copy safe, even though there were no details in our files about new identities. Those affidavits, though, they were explosive and put six men in grave danger of prison or worse. If it were up to me, I would choose worse.

We attended Julie Bates's funeral. It was a very sad day. Her mother Lucy was beside herself. When we greeted her at the viewing the night before, she kept repeating that a child should not die before the mother. I would add no one should have to die like Julie had, either.

The funeral was held in a nondenominational chapel on the grounds of Llano cemetery. The minister was dressed in a black suit, no liturgical robes in sight. Not that he would ask me, but I agreed with his choice of attire. There was no place for opulence amidst the depths of despair.

Deputy Sheriff Rob Bates made a grand entrance, along with colleagues from the Kingsland County Sheriff's Office, and the police departments of Horseshoe Bay, Marble Falls, and Granite Falls. I didn't know them but merely observed the uniform shoulder patches. I did recognize the Granite Falls cop that stopped Mary Louise and I returning from dinner; Beverley, I believe was his name. In a manner of speaking, he had warned me of bad people in town. This was after my two encounters with Deputy Bates, and my small tirade in Sheriff Holmes's office in Kingsland County. I didn't understand if Beverley was a good guy warning me to be careful, or a bad guy just warning me in general.

The funeral was short and sweet, after which we all proceeded out to the burial plot. The day was cold and overcast. I have been to a number of funerals, and burying a loved one on a sunny day just never seemed right to me. The minister said a few more kind words, and after the usual "ashes to ashes, dust to dust," it was over.

The reception was at Hill Country Medical Center, generously donated by Dr. Buck Owens. There were several auditoriums on the first level, and the largest had been chosen. Lucy and Julie had lived in the area all their lives, so many more attended the reception than the funeral. Eating and drinking somehow mitigate the pain of losing someone you cared about. Nothing like a good old-fashioned Irish wake, if you ask me.

Buck motioned Mary Louise over to a corner after we had a beverage in hand.

"Have you had any time to review the documents I gave you?"

"We read them thoroughly several times. Mary Louise had a safe installed yesterday morning, and that's where we're storing them. They are pretty explosive."

"That they are. You're probably wondering how we made these women disappear, and where they are, and who they are now."

"Of course," said Mary Louise, "but we don't want to endanger them or ourselves any further."

"I would never intentionally put you in danger. I thought you might want to know, as a matter of intellectual curiosity. But I would never consider giving the new identities of these woman to anyone. Only Mads and I have this information, and I don't think Mads's security is current, so I plan to retrieve those documents from her and keep them with mine. Those will be the only copies, safe and secure. When is a good time to meet? I think we should show you two our little operation, then proceed over to Mourning Doves for a look at our rescue facilities."

"I've got patients scheduled along with a few surgeries the rest of the week, so maybe on Saturday?"

"Mary Louise?"

"That works for me, Buck."

"Fine. Saturday at ten in the morning. See you then," he said, and walked off to greet a friend.

"We could have met Friday. You're not working . . ."

"That's a sacred golf day. Chuck the real estate guy asked me to join his Friday group, so I'm playing the cruelest sport on the planet on Friday."

"Interesting. His wife asked me to play in her group that day as well, so I'll be looking for that one good shot out of ninety-plus."

The rest of the week was uneventful with respect to work. I saw patients, did a few surgeries, all at an unusually relaxed pace for me. I was happy with my decision to opt for a slower kind of life as an orthopedic surgeon. I felt after one week that I could spend more time with the patients, get to know them a little better, and still maintain a high level of care without rushing from patient to patient and case to case.

The Friday golf game could have gone better, had I played better. I have to admit, I was a little rusty, having spent an inordinate amount of time on the missing-women cases. After Mary Louise and I toured the facilities at HCMC that were in some way particular for the women that Buck had called "our women," and after visiting Mourning Doves, I planned to return to a somewhat normal life here in Granite Falls. Truth was, I didn't know what a normal life here was yet. We had just moved into a new home, I had started a small orthopedic practice, and in the midst of all that I had involved myself in six cases of missing women that turned out not to be missing at all, just relocated to a different, and hopefully safer, environment. The idea that I was solely responsible for maintaining these women's voices through my investigative efforts was a sham. According to Buck, they had gone on to new lives and were safe and secure. Regardless, I still had many questions for my mentor, but at least I could relax, knowing that the runaways' voices did not need to be heard. In fact, just the opposite. They more likely than not wanted to remain hidden and silent.

We met Buck at ten as agreed. Lucy was off on Saturday, so we helped ourselves to bottles of water and pastries that Buck had supplied. After the requisite time to make small talk, eat, and wipe the crumbs off my shirt and jacket, we ventured out of the conference room and past Buck's private office to two shiny wooden doors with large brass handles. Buck took a key from his pocket, turned the lock, and opened both doors toward us.

We stepped into a large closet with a built-in desk that contained multiple rolled-up architectural plans. Once unfurled, the sketches showed two sections of a large room. On one side were half a dozen operating tables, complete with anesthesia machines, overhead lights, and various small but elevated tables that could be used for surgical instruments. On the opposite side of the room were stations much like you see in a hair salon or backstage at a concert or play. There were a dozen or so of these cubicles, each with a large mirror and a chair in front. To me these stations would be appropriate for applying makeup, changing hair color, plucking eyebrows, eyeliner tattooing, and cutting and styling hair. Alongside each mirror and chair was an elevated table, each laden with combs, brushes, and scissors for applying a stylist's trade.

"What do you think?" Buck asked.

"Looks like an upscale beauty salon," offered Mary Louise.

"And well-stocked operating rooms built with an open concept. What about sterility?" I asked.

Buck drew my attention to the upper part of the diagram of the main room. "These are rolling shades that will seal off the operating side of the space. We should be able to schedule procedures in such a way as not to have an operation going while a makeover proceeds nearby. At any rate, there are always a few kinks to be worked out."

As we exited the closet, I saw a small figure walking toward us from the rear of the facility. It was Sister Mads. I extended my hand. She hugged me instead. She was so short, I had to lean down like I was embracing a child.

"And this is your lovely bride?" she asked.

"I'm Mary Louise Brady."

Sister Mads hugged her also.

"How's the arm?" I asked.

"Better every day, Doc. Thanks to you. What do you think about our facility plans here? Pretty uptown, wouldn't you say?"

"Well, I'm impressed. The drawings depict a fancy MASH unit, except for the beauty salon/barber shop on the other side," I responded.

She looked at her benefactor. "Have you explained what it is we're doing here, Buck?"

"No, Mads. I was saving that for you."

"Mary Louise, Buck told me that you had worked a hotline in Houston for the women's center, so you have first-hand knowledge about what we're up against. But your husband here probably does not. I'm going to give him the spiel. If I bore you or Buck, well, sorry, but that's just too bad. The work we're doing here is far too important.

"A women's shelter is a place of temporary refuge and support for women trying to escape domestic violence. The CDC has published statistics that show one in three women will experience physical violence during their lifetime. Women's shelters across the country help individuals escape, and they act as a place of protection as women choose how to move forward with their lives. Some shelters offer advanced support, such as counseling, medical and legal guidance, and skill workshops to help women move on independently. Many of the women who are victims of domestic violence have children in tow, which complicates matters significantly.

"The ability for these women to escape is valuable to their sense of self-worth. Also, many of these women have limited financial options, and shelters can provide tangible resources—like money—to help them establish a new life. Do you realize that many of these women become homeless because they are financially dependent on their abuser?

"One of the first women's shelters in the country was established around 1972 in California by a local group of women who attended the same church. A friend of mine was a founding member, which is how I got involved. Originally, these abused runaways were housed in volunteers' homes. As time went on, and I took my vows and entered the convent in Austin, I established a shelter within the Church and was able to house and provide services to these women on a limited scale. My budget was such that we could never afford to provide all the care they needed. We had funding from the State of Texas, from the federal government, and from private donations as well as from the Church, but it was never enough.

"Do you folks realize that there are somewhere between five and ten thousand abused women in need that go without help each and every day in our country because of space or lack-of-funding issues? It's a crime, is what it is. As a result, my old friend Buck Owens and I hatched a plan, and what you're seeing in these plans is a dream coming to fruition. We couldn't fulfill our dreams of this separate facility at the outset, but in time, with donations, we'll be able to create this space. We'll go to Mourning Doves and see my side of the operation shortly. Questions?"

"Where did the name come from—Mourning Doves?"

"The spelling is 'mourning' and not 'morning' doves. Doves make a cooing sound, which can be construed as a sad, mourning sort of sound. Doves are a symbol of peace. They are biblical. Remember that in the Old Testament a dove was released by Noah after the flood to find land? And it came back with an olive leaf, signifying a sign of life? And in the New Testament, a dove is used as a symbol of the Holy Spirit and is an emblem of innocence and purity. That's what we're dealing with here. Sad doves being abused by satanic and evil men," said Sister Mads.

"Mary Louise? Your thoughts?" Buck asked.

"Well, from the drawings of the operating tables and the makeover cubicles, it appears that you're not only providing housing and counseling to these abused women, you're planning to change them physically. Would that be an accurate description?"

"Excellent," said Sister Mads. "That's exactly what we're beginning to do. We're hiding them in plain sight!"

CHAPTER 28

MOURNING DOVES

We four got in Buck's car, drove to his home, and parked in the garage. We walked through the house, then outside onto the deck, got in his powerboat, and headed across the lake to Mourning Doves.

"Isn't there a front entrance?" I yelled at Sister Mads over the roar of the engines.

"No. Too dangerous," she answered. "There was at one time, allowing us to complete the house and move in the furniture and appliances, but once that was done, we built an eight-foot wall around the front and both sides of the house. The only entrance is by boat. We had some break-ins early on, men looking for their wives in order to take them back home."

"What about deliveries and such?"

"And who would be accepting deliveries at the house? One of the women hiding from abusive husbands and significant others? And to what name would the goods be shipped? Their old names? Or their new names? C'mon, Doc, we're trying to keep these women hidden, and give them new lives. Should we just take out an ad in the *Highlander* and announce their presence? And before you ask, all mail is delivered to an anonymous post office box in Horseshoe Bay."

I had asked some questions, not appreciating the lengths to which Sister Mads had gone to protect the identities of "her" women.

Buck navigated the boat into a boat slip adjacent to two covered moorings housing boats that appeared to be part of the Mourning Doves complex. One was a speedboat, not unlike the one we came over in, the other a twenty-one-foot Duffy electric boat, which could hold twelve passengers. We climbed out onto the large redwood deck, faded to gray as most decks are due to exposure to sun and lake water. We made several turns through elevation changes and arrived at two massive sliding doors. I saw a couple of women that appeared to be doing yard work of some sort off to the side of the house. They both wore denim pants and long-sleeve shirts and sported large straw hats that covered most of their faces. I don't think I would recognize my wife in that disguise.

Mads slid the doors back, and we entered a great room. It had dark wood rafters with horizontal beams. I noted several women bustling about, cleaning, sweeping, vacuuming, all in the same outfits as the two ladies outside, but without the straw hats. There was a large industrial kitchen off to the side, open to the great room. There were three women there, and from the aromas coming from the area, they were cooking delicious dishes. Walking nearby, I noted double sinks, double ovens, double dishwashers, and double microwaves. Three meals a day for twenty people must require a lot of kitchen appliances.

We passed through the great room into a large hallway that ran perpendicular to the great room. The hallway made a ninety-degree turn at each end and ran back toward the front of the house. Each side hallway led to five large bedrooms in a row, and each bedroom had two queen beds and a private bath, so ten bedrooms in all. The structure could house twenty women. I wondered where Sister Mads slept but thought that unimportant in this situation. There was no garage, so no cars to worry about. The house was basically a great room, a kitchen, and ten bedrooms, with a large rear deck and two boats. I also wondered about fire department access in case of fire, but then realized these women had much more to worry about than a fire. The lake was nearby and provided an easy escape using the two boats, which in my estimation held well over twenty people together. Still, they had to have passed some sort of building inspection. I wondered how much of this operation had been forced to walk the tightrope of legality.

As we walked, I observed that all the women I encountered kept their heads bowed and their faces turned away from the group. They did not offer any sort of greeting, not even a nod. They had to know that Sister Mads would only bring friends into the house, but I presume they all had been trained to be wary of all strangers.

"Any questions?" asked Mads.

"We've seen the bedroom arrangements here and see that twenty women can be cared for at one time. Buck told us that the stay is two months. Is there the possibility for longer stays if need be?" I asked.

"Yes," answered Mads. "We've had women stay here up to six months in extenuating circumstances, but that's the max. Sometimes these women we take in are so battered physically that they have developed post-traumatic stress disorder. Those ladies require more counseling and, well, more of all our services we offer—medical, legal, financial. All these women have PTSD to some degree, but some are so damaged I'm not sure they can ever totally recover. But we do our best."

"We've seen the beginning of your program here at Mourning Doves. I presume you re-introduce your patients into a normal lifestyle setting, then provide counseling services in the various disciplines that they would require to function on their own again. Then, sometime between two and six months, they go out on their own. What kind of decision-making process is involved in who gets what, or do all these women get the benefit of both non-invasive cosmetic changes and significant surgical modifications to their physical appearance?"

I thought those were good questions from Mary Louise.

"Buck, you might want to tackle that," Mads responded.

"As you might imagine, it's a complicated issue. We learned early on that leaving an abuser is the most dangerous time for a victim of domestic violence. One study found that in men who have killed their spouses, the precipitating factor was the threat of separation or the actual separation. We found that a significant percentage of abused women returned to their abuser, even after a lengthy stay in a shelter, for a number of complex reasons, but amongst those are the threats by the abuser: the abuser will kill the woman and/or the kids, they will win custody of the kids, they will kill family members or pets, they will ruin the woman financially. It comes down to a matter of control by the abuser.

"With that in mind, we—meaning me, Sister Mads, and a few others who were instrumental in starting this program—searched our souls for something we could do to change those statistics. What could we do to encourage women to leave an abusive situation and to stay gone? We decided that if we could change the woman on the inside and give her the courage and ability to stand on her own two feet, why couldn't we change her on the outside as well?

"Early on, we experimented with easy changes, such as hair-style, hair color, lipstick shades, texture and tint of cosmetics and lipsticks. We added glasses or converted from glasses to contacts. We changed their style of dress as well, and those modifications improved the overall statistics of women who did not return to their abusers. But it wasn't enough. Mads and I had the idea to permanently change their looks through plastic and dental surgery. We started with rhinoplasties and proceeded to facelifts, ear tucks, and blepharoplasties, then added dental implants and mandibular osteotomies for overbites and underbites. If you combine these physical changes with the psychological changes, you essentially have created a new woman.

"We had to take a number of people into our confidence to make the project work. Nurses, doctors, dentists, and cosmetologists were involved and sworn to secrecy. Each had a small piece of the puzzle, but only Mads and I knew all the details. We decided to provide the total alteration process to one woman every other month. We chose women who were mentally strong, had jobs and their own checking accounts, and had the ability to disappear without the fear of losing small children or neglecting aging parents they were responsible for. We also chose women who had frequented HCMC with physical problems that could be abuse-related.

"The first was Margaret Harris. She was perfect. No kids. Dispatcher at a trucking company. The only fly in the ointment was her husband, who's a detective with Granite Falls Police Department. We figured we might as well give it a go, because if a cop couldn't find his wife, the average abusive husband couldn't. We had pinned a lot of hope on those spousal agreements we had created, but we knew better than to fully trust that these abusive men would abide by them. She was fine for a year, but we got worried when you recognized her working at Chico's as a store clerk. If her husband happened to go into that store, would he know her? You did, and only from a photograph. We convinced her to move to another location, not so close to the lake area.

"Then there was Katie Smith, an event planner at the resort, two grown kids, husband a dentist. After Katie came Carla Robinson, a nurse at the hospital, one daughter a senior in college, and a truck-driving husband. Next was Karen Statton, another nurse at the hospital, a son in medical school, husband a Ferguson engineer. Then we freed Jorja Watson, a real estate agent with her husband and who had no kids. And lastly, Hilary Allen, banker with a lawyer husband, and a son working with her, a daughter in law school, and a son a senior in college. All women with minimal encumbrances.

"We had a seventh disappearance planned: Julie Bates. We had her all prepped and ready to go. Her mother, Lucy Williams, my admin assistant, was in on the transformation process. But the night before, she was run over by a speeding auto as she was walking out of a movie. Her mother says Julie swore the husband pushed her into the oncoming vehicle. Whether he had an inkling of what was to happen the next day and was trying to halt her departure, or he's just a malicious son of a bitch, we don't know. Nonetheless, she's now deceased, victim of a violent rape/murder, which to my way of thinking smells of Rob Bates, her deputy sheriff husband.

"That's our story, and you two are officially on board. You are of course sworn to secrecy about all our work for all time."

"I have a question, Buck."

"Sure, Jim."

"Are these the only women in the program who have had the full treatment? Just six?"

"Yes. We've gone through partial transformations in different combinations with a number of different women, but only these six received the total benefit of our expertise. You realize that this includes an identity change with all the trimmings—birth certificate, driver's license, voter registration, a credit card, and $25,000 in cash. All these women are working and are productive citizens, hiding under new identities. Those who have children, parents, or siblings long for a reunion, but that's just not possible as long as their abusive husbands are still alive. Remember, Mads and I have the only comprehensive data revealing these women's new identities and locations. And by the way, Sister, I want to pick up your copies today and put them with mine. I don't trust your security."

"I'll show you my security," and she walked to a hall closet and pulled out a Purdie twelve-gauge side-by-side shotgun.

"Nonetheless, Mads, I'm taking all the paperwork to the safety deposit box at the bank. I'll keep my set in my office safe. It's virtually impenetrable."

She reluctantly put away the shotgun, walked down the bedroom hallway, and returned shortly with a large file folder. She handed the paperwork to Buck, and we left the facility, took the boat to Buck's house, and returned to HCMC.

CHAPTER 29

GRANITE FALLS POLICE

By the time we'd finished our tour of Mourning Doves, it was two in the afternoon. We weren't sure we were hungry, but alcohol was definitely in our near future. We drove to the Lantana Grill, sat at the bar, and ordered a Bloody Mary for each of us. We were quiet until the drinks arrived.

"What's the verdict?" I asked her.

"I am almost speechless. Do you think what they are doing is legal?"

"You mean, taking a battered woman out of her abusive situation, giving her a physical and mental makeover, and providing her with a new identity in another location? I think not only is it legal, but it qualifies Buck and Sister Mads for sainthood, not that she isn't qualified already by having become a nun and being married to Jesus in the Church's eyes."

"I'm thinking of all the other women that don't have it so good. If Sister takes in twenty women every two months, and only one is selected for—what would we call it? A transformation?— what becomes of the other nineteen? And I wonder what their success rate has been since inception? She's been open maybe four years? There were many women that passed through that facility prior to this new process, and during the past year, another one hundred and fourteen or so, not including the totally transformed ones.

"There must have been something like three hundred and sixty women at the facility over the three years prior to the new process. What happened to all those women? Did they escape their abuser, or return to their same situation as before? And what happened to all the children of the other women? Sister doesn't allow kids in the facility, so they had to either stay with the husband or get farmed out to grandparents or other relatives. Don't get me wrong, I'm in awe of what Mourning Doves is doing, but I can't stop thinking of all those other women."

"Don't you think that's the way it is in all other shelters? A few make it, but most do not? I have no experience with this problem. This . . . situation? Disease? Issue? . . . is a problem that permeates all levels of society. Buck and Mads have developed a solution of sorts, available, however, to only a tiny minority of affected women. I would think saving one woman is better than saving no women. And maybe what they are offering saves many more women than you and I realize."

"You could be right, Jim Bob. I regret that I am more disturbed by those who aren't helped in the long-term than I rejoice in the few that are transformed into new identities."

"I don't remember who said this, either Mads or Buck, but they admit they are unable to help everyone. They help who they can, and leave the rest to . . . chance. Divine guidance. I have no idea, Mary Louise, of the answers to your questions about those left behind. You should visit more with Mads."

Discussing the women who did not make the cut for a transformation reminded me of the patient I had seen in my office with the fractured humerus. She seemed to have minimal personality, and her husband acted in a somewhat aggressive manner about when his injured wife could return to her "chores." Was she a victim as well? Or was I becoming paranoid? I needed to get her name and review her medical records.

After the Bloody Mary we were hungry, so we placed orders for medium-rare cheeseburgers, and we ate with gusto. We stopped by the hospital on the way home, and I took Mary Louise up to my new office. I'd almost forgotten she had decorated it in my absence but thought she might want to see it again. Shelly Wood was at a desk in the nursing/secretarial pool cubicles and stood to greet us. She had already met Mary Louise during the office makeover.

"Shelly, I can't believe you're here on a Saturday afternoon."

"I'm working the ER tonight and I thought I would come up and catch up on paperwork before my shift. Speaking of Saturday, what are you doing here?"

"I saw a patient a few days back, maybe Tuesday, with a broken humerus. Do you remember her?"

"Yes, Doctor. What about her?"

"I'd like to see her medical records."

She stared at me for a moment, then left the area to pull the patient's chart. Charts and medical records were kept in a central area on the physicians' office floor. Since all records were subject to electronic data entry, I didn't know what was available in paper and what had to be printed from the computer. I knew there was a giant printer in that area with the capability to copy hundreds of pages in a few minutes.

"I printed her office visit and X-ray report for you. If you want more than just that visit, I'll have to go back and print other medical records. She's been a patient here a number of times."

That piqued my interest. "Would it be too much trouble to print what we have, including ER visits and other doctor visits?"

"No sir, just give me a few minutes."

Mary Louise and I sat in my office, made small talk, and admired the tasteful work she had done to make the space my own. We also were mesmerized by the Hill Country views. There were a couple of Blanco County summits in the distance, called the Twin Sisters. It was said to be a premium view and a sign of good fortune when the Twin Sisters were in the background.

Shelly returned with a stack of paper. She placed it on my desk and returned to work at hers. I scanned the records and noted that Bonnie McLellan had been in the ER five times in the past two years for various injuries. She had sustained an ankle fracture, a collarbone fracture, a couple of broken ribs, and a mandible, or jawbone, fracture. Surgery had been required for the ankle injury, so she spent the night in the hospital. The other visits were as an outpatient. On each occasion the person who had brought her in was her husband Seth. His employer was listed as self-employed, but with no explanation as to what he did.

I thanked Shelly for her time, told her I would see her Monday, and departed for home.

When we pulled into the street leading to the gate that protected the four houses in our enclave, we noticed a car sitting off to the side. We entered the gate code and pulled into our driveway, and we saw the dark-blue sedan slip in behind us and pull in front of our house. I jumped out of the Tahoe and headed to the offending vehicle to let the driver know in no uncertain terms that this was a private drive and private property, and that they were trespassing. Two people exited the car, both with suits, one with a tie. They extended their arms, holding badges.

"Dr. Brady?" the driver said.

Cops. "Yes. How can I help you?"

"I'm Det. Sly Baldwin, and this is my partner, Det. Norma Raymond. We're with the Granite Falls Police Department. We'd like to ask you some questions about the murder of Julie Bates. May we step inside? I don't want your neighbors to hear our discussion."

I led them inside and introduced them to Mary Louise. We offered them a beverage; they accepted bottled waters.

"What a view," offered Det. Baldwin. "How long have you lived here?"

"Only a couple of months."

"I understand you're a new doctor at Hill Country Medical Center. How's that going for you?"

"It's going well, thanks. I worked in Houston for many years in the same capacity, orthopedic surgeon, and came here to retire. I'm working part-time currently. What can I do for you?"

"We're investigating the murder of Julie Bates. I understand you knew her well?"

"I can't say that I knew her well. I repaired a broken hip and pelvis she sustained when a car ran into her when she was coming out of the movies. She also had a broken forearm which a colleague repaired. I saw her at the request of her mother, Lucy Williams, who is the administrative assistant for Dr. Buck Owens, chairman and CEO of HCMC. I fixed Julie's hip and followed her recovery in the hospital until we returned to Houston; we were still living there at the time. I returned a couple of weeks later and removed her sutures. She was accepted into the rehab program at HCMC, which gave her an additional four weeks of healing time under supervision of nurses and physical therapists. It was a devastating injury and she required a good deal of postoperative care."

"During the time Mrs. Bates was in the rehab section, did she have an injury to the operated area?" asked Baldwin.

I was hesitant to implicate Julie's husband, not knowing the relationship between him and these officers. However, the truth shall set you free.

"Yes. She said her husband, Kingsland County Deputy Sheriff Rob Bates, came into her room early in the morning, got into an argument with her, and pounded the incisional area around her hip and pelvis with his fists. Julie started screaming, and the nurse on duty ran into the room, but Julie was alone. The nurse didn't see Deputy Bates. I of course wasn't there, so I can't validate his presence either. Julie was insistent that he was present and beat her hip with his fists, however."

"But no one else saw him, as far as you know, sir?"

"That's my understanding."

"We've interviewed Deputy Bates, and he swears he wasn't present and feels his wife made up the story to shine a bad light on him. What do you think?"

"I can't say. I have had a couple of run-ins with Bates, not of my choosing." I related to the detectives the incident in the parking garage of the condo the evening of Julie's surgery and my rescue by hotel security. I also explained his accosting me on the highway for alleged speeding, and my rescue by the Horseshoe Bay patrolman in the speed trap. I also told the officers about the HSB officer making a comment about Bates's reputation.

"I ran into him one other time, in the parking lot of HCMC, after Julie died. I never got what he was doing there. I was carrying some files out to my car, and he seemed very interested in what was in my possession. I extended my condolences for his wife. That was about it."

"Did you know that Lucy Williams, Julie's mother, accused Deputy Bates of pushing Julie into the moving vehicle that struck her?"

"Yes. She told me that her daughter told her that's how she came to be injured."

"We've interviewed Bates twice. He left us the impression that his deceased wife wanted attention, and she manufactured these injuries, especially the one in the hospital. He told us that the perp that ran her down outside the movie theatre was speeding and high on PCP, and that he had nothing to do with that injury except to aid his wife in getting to the hospital."

There was no comment I could make about either of those accusations.

"Norma, do you have any questions for the good doctor?"

"Dr. Brady, what is your general impression of Deputy Bates? Good guy? Bad guy?"

I hesitated for a moment. "I sense he has a mean streak and loves wielding the power of the badge. Whether he injured his wife on either occasion, I couldn't say."

The detectives stood and shook our hands, thanked us for our time, and left.

I looked at Mary Louise. She said, "Some retirement."

We walked Tip out the security gate for our subdivision and down the lane that led to a main thoroughfare that ran east to west, accessing several restaurants, a spa, and eventually the Hill Country Resort. We walked for a while and enjoyed watching Tip chase birds and smell the odors of the region. Just before dusk, we made a 180-degree turn, walked back uphill, and got back to our deck before sunset. We had an eastern view from the deck, and a peekaboo western view through the woods in the front of the house. We took two lawn chairs and walked out to the end of our property where we could witness the sun melting away into an orange and red pool. The evening cooled quickly and we were exhausted from the day's activities, so we turned in early.

"Jim Bob?" Mary Louise said, as we lay in bed watching an episode of *Breaking Bad*.

"Yes?"

"Are you going to rest tomorrow and gather your wits about you in preparation for your next day of real work on Monday?"

"Yes I am, my dear."

"And you're going to be a very good boy tomorrow and not go chasing after missing women who aren't really missing, and you're going to avoid getting on the bad side of law enforcement?"

"Mary Louise, that's exactly my intent. I'm looking forward to the calm." I left out 'before the storm' because I liked where the conversation was headed.

She got out of bed and stood facing away from me. I could tell she was unbuttoning her pajama top, which she promptly laid gently over a nearby chair. She then slowly removed her pajama bottoms and turned and faced me in all her glory. It was quite a sight, and I was already, shall we say, at attention. She crawled back into bed, rolled on top of me, and gave me a lusty open-mouthed kiss. I started to say something clever, but she said, "No talking." Fine with me.

CHAPTER 30

BACK TO WORK

Sunday went as God intended . . .a day of rest. We cooked bacon, sausage, eggs, hash browns, and sourdough toast. We shared a split of Veuve Clicquot champagne. We took the Tipster for another long walk, then drove to Austin for an early movie and a late sushi lunch. I was so tempted to walk into Chico's and see if the Margaret Harris look-alike was working, but things between Mary Louise and I were improving so much that our brief separation was a dim memory. I definitely didn't want to rock the boat. Besides, Buck had indicated Margaret was moving farther away. We saw and thoroughly enjoyed a Clint Eastwood production and dined on excellent sushi. The remainder of Sunday we spent at home, watching football, napping, and eating leftover sushi.

I was up at 5 a.m. Monday morning, then showered, made coffee, and was at the hospital by 6:15. I had two virgin hip replacements to do. When I had started performing regular surgeries here, I briefly wondered how I would fare with two nurses and myself, having had an assistant or two in the operating room for most of my career. I shouldn't have worried. The two were a scrub nurse, whose job it was to pass instruments and parts needed for the operation from her table to me, and a nurse who was assisting me. Both were very experienced, and the surgeries went smoothly.

I also discovered something very interesting. In my former life and job, I ran two operating rooms. When I was finished with the "meat" of the procedure, I would go to the next room and let the resident or fellow wash out the wound and close. There was no one around to do that in my current situation, so after each prosthesis was inserted and the tension in the room had subsided, I spent the relaxed closure time getting to know the nurses and the anesthesia staff. And it was quite pleasant. I realized I had missed a great deal of camaraderie over the years, rushing from room to room.

I did the usual duties after surgery, dictating operative reports and talking to the families. I had a bite of lunch and walked across the parking lot to my office. I found Shelly Wood there, on the phone making appointments, it sounded like. There were a few items for me to sign on my desk, but nothing like I was used to in the old days at University Medical Center. Back then, I spent a great deal of time dictating reports or talking to insurance company clerks and the occasional physician, justifying surgical procedures that my patients needed. I hadn't been around Hill Country Medical Center that long, but there was none of that here. Perhaps HCMC had some sort of proprietary relationship with the insurance companies, and surgical procedures were approved posthaste. At any rate, whatever the reason, that was a huge advantage and time saver.

"Would you mind seeing a patient? I know office hours are Tuesday and Thursday, but—"

"Of course. Who is it?"

"Coincidentally, it's Bonnie McLellan, the humerus fracture you inquired about Saturday."

"What's wrong?"

"She said increased pain. She called me this morning, so I told her to come in after your surgeries. I put her in the cast room."

I walked down the stairs to the cast room accompanied by Shelly and saw Bonnie in the corner talking to Jake, the head of the casting/splinting department.

"Hello, Bonnie. What's the problem? Shelly said you had increased pain?"

"Yes, Dr. Brady. It's almost more than I can bear."

Her husband Seth was standing nearby. I nodded at him. He stared at me.

I looked at her arm. It was black and blue. Her hand was swollen to about twice normal size.

"Jake, can you X-ray—"

"Done. Take a look."

We walked over to the viewing box, and what was once a simple spiral fracture of the humerus was now a displaced fracture with, unless I missed them last visit, two additional horizontal fragments. One was pointed and clearly was interfering with the circulation.

"Bonnie, has this arm had any additional trauma since I saw you?"

"I did fall once, Doctor. I put out my wrist to catch my fall, and I heard something inside snap."

"This isn't good. Your circulation is impaired. You have what we call a compartment syndrome. I'm going to have to go in and release the pressure. I might have to internally fixate the fractures while I'm there. Also, I have to call in a vascular surgeon."

"Now hold on just a minute, Doctor," said Seth. "We don't want no operation. You said that arm would be fine healin' on its own."

"That was then, this is now, sir. Your wife could lose that arm. You come with us and sign the papers if she can't. Let's go."

The staff had the OR ready in less than thirty minutes. I was introduced to Dr. Michael Reardon, cardiac and vascular surgeon. He agreed she could lose the arm if we didn't intervene. We scrubbed in, draped the patient, who was already asleep and prepped, and went to work. I let Dr. Reardon make the incision to expose the brachial artery, which was partially occluded by the fracture fragment as well as about a pound of clotted blood in the arm. He gently ran a suction catheter up and down the arm from the shoulder to the elbow, evacuating the blood clots. Bonnie's hand began to pink up almost immediately, so knowing now that we could save the arm, the tension in the room abated somewhat.

The artery was not lacerated and didn't require repair, so Reardon turned the procedure over to me. I was able to apply a plate and multiple screws to the fracture to stabilize it. That spiky piece of bone that was occluding the artery was not a supporting fragment, so I removed it, minced it, and used it for bone graft in and around the fracture site.

Reardon returned when I was about to close the wound. He checked the artery and was pleased the offending spike was gone and happy with the stability of the upper arm.

"Nice work," he said. "Let's do it again sometime."

I closed the wound, applied a dressing and a splint, and went out to the waiting room to speak to Mr. McLellan.

"Your wife is very lucky, sir. A little longer and she would have lost her arm. How in the world did she fall with enough force to break a bone that was already broken?"

"Well, she's a little clumsy," he said.

I was very suspicious about the injury, both of them in fact, maybe legitimately or maybe influenced by my involvement with missing and abused women.

"She'll be here for a few days until we're sure she's out of the woods. When she gets home, she has to be very careful. Do you understand me, sir?"

"Sure, Doc, we'll take good care of her."

I had my doubts about that.

When I arrived at home, there was an unfamiliar vehicle in our one guest parking spot. I was pleased to see Susan Beeson talking with Mary Louise when I entered the house. I hugged both ladies and asked Susan what she was doing back here so soon.

"I took the job with the FBI in the Austin district. I'm the new ASAC—Assistant Special Agent in Charge."

"That was quick. What about school for Gene Jr., and Gene Sr.'s job?"

"I'm going to commute until school is out. If time and circumstances permit, I'll go back to Houston on Friday afternoons and return here on Monday mornings. Gene Jr. will finish his school year in May. Gene Sr. is a CPA as you know, and he's not ready to retire. He can either commute for a while, as in come here on weekends, or maybe he'll be able to handle his clients and live here. This is the modern age of telecommunication. He tells me it's rare to have face time with a client other than Skype, except during the initial meeting. Or he might find a job he likes in this area. We'll see. Anyway, the Houston house is for sale, and I'm here looking for real estate, somewhere between Granite Falls and Austin."

"Austin traffic has become a nightmare, so you might want to look close to work."

"The new FBI office is on the far west side of town, so that does give me some options. We're only thirty or forty minutes away, according to my calculations."

"That's correct," said Mary Louise. "But if you go north toward Barton Creek or Lake Travis, that'll add time to your commute. It all depends on what you want to enjoy when you're not working. Here in the Lake LBJ area, it's golfing and boating. In Austin, it's fine dining and good music on Sixth Street or at Austin City Limits. You might want to rent for a while, get a feel for both."

"Good advice. I'm going to look around here for a day or two, then I'll go back to Austin and do the same process there. Meanwhile, I'll get involved in the active cases in the Austin office and see where that leads. I'm really excited about the new job."

"And we're glad that you're glad," said Mary Louise.

We took Susan to the yacht club for a celebratory dinner and toasted to past and future good times.

CHAPTER 31

BONNIE

Tuesday brought new patients, a plethora of folks needing hip and knee replacements. The patients tended to be older than I was used to in terms of age, but not in terms of physical health. Most of the folks in the Lakes area were golfers, and those who weren't, used to be, and walked for exercise. I couldn't prove it, but my impression was that my patients in Houston tended to less active than patients in the Hill Country, had joint replacements earlier in life, and were seeking repeat procedures. My new Lake patients tended to be seeking virgin replacements at an older age. My explanation for this conundrum was weather. Living in good weather tends to produce more outdoor activity. More outdoor activities produce better overall physical health. Houston was rainy and humid. The Hill Country was arid and dry. As an illustration, I had a 90-year-old man come in who played golf four days a week, walked the other three days, and simply wanted a refill of his arthritis medicine. He said surgery to replace a joint was silly. He was happy with what the good Lord gave him, and he would go to the grave with his original body parts. So there, Father Time . . .

I made rounds early that morning before clinic began. I was worried about Bonnie McLellan's circulation. It was fine and she was sleeping, so I chose not to disturb her. After clinic, I made a repeat visit to once again check on her hand circulation. This time she was awake, and her husband Seth was not present.

"How's the pain level, Bonnie?"

"Much better, Dr. Brady. I guess I was in real trouble, huh?"

"Yes, ma'am, you were. I'm glad you came in when you did."

"Well, I thought it would get better, but . . . oh well, live and learn."

"Bonnie, I wanted to discuss an issue with you, and since Seth isn't here, this seems like a good time."

She stared at the sheets and didn't answer.

"You've been a patient here a number of times for multiple fractures, more than most people would be expected to have unless you have some sort of bone disease I don't know about. Do you?"

"No sir, not that I know of."

"So, one conclusion we could draw is that you're terribly clumsy and unlucky. A more logical explanation is that you're being abused by someone, most likely your husband."

She started to shake, then whimper, then sob. I handed her some tissues.

"I can refer you to Social Services, see if they can get you some help."

"Dr. Brady, I have my mother living with us. She's old and can't take care of herself. I have to think of her. Seth lets her live in our house. He doesn't like it and takes it out on me sometimes."

"Bonnie, taking it out on you by breaking your bones is not exactly what I would call stellar behavior on the part of your husband. If that's what is happening, you can file criminal charges against him, get you out of the house, and—"

"Oh, no, Dr. Brady. Mother and I are totally dependent on Seth financially. Whatever situation we're in, we're pretty much stuck with."

"I would disagree, Bonnie. I know of an organization called Mourning Doves, and their purpose is to rescue women such as yourself, put them in a different location, and get them away from their abusers."

"They won't take me back."

"What? You mean you've been there?"

"Yes, a few years ago, when Mother still lived independently. I stayed with them for two months. I had all sorts of counseling, and I was exposed to programs I could get involved in to help me out of my situation, but the bottom line was that I had no marketable skills for employment. I could not make a living on my own. And I really thought that after two months, Seth would appreciate me more and wouldn't hurt me again. Turns out I was wrong. After a few months, I contacted the lady that ran the program, and she wouldn't let me return. That's their rule. If you go back to the situation you were in before you entered the program, you can't return. It's like strike one and you're out. Thanks for being so kind to me, and for fixing my arm, but I'm stuck where I am."

I discussed the conversation I had with Bonnie with Mary Louise when I got home.

"It's very sad, Jim Bob, but not unusual in my experience. It's a sad and tired old story, but the story just seems to repeat itself time and time again. It sounds to me like Sister Mads's policy is not to waste time on someone who is not going to leave their abuser. She gives them one chance, and if they return to their original situation, she won't give them another. In her defense, Mourning Doves spends a lot of money on their residents and probably can't afford to try and redeem a woman who returns to her abusive situation. There is only so much money, and there are so many women waiting for a chance to get out from under their abuser and make a better life for themselves. Some women, for many reasons, just cannot be helped. As a result, organizations such as Mourning Doves have to spend their resources on those that have the best chance of survival outside their abusive environment. It's sad, it's tragic, and it seems so wrong, but it's just a fact of life. That's one of the reasons I got off the hotline in Houston. My frustration level got so high dealing with impossible situations, I felt like I was beating my head against the wall. I hated myself for giving up, but I just couldn't deal with it any longer. I don't know how Sister Mads does it."

I was quiet. There were no words to express what each of us was feeling.

"By the way, Lucy Williams called. Buck wants us to attend the monthly board meeting of Mourning Doves. It's tomorrow night."

"Are you sure you want to get involved? After what you just explained about the hotline experience, do you think it's wise or an exercise in futility?"

"Well, Jim Bob, I'm willing to go to the meeting, meet the board members, and get the lay of the land. See what their expectations are, see what their long-term goals are, see how they approach successes and failures, see what has happened to the other women over the last few years who weren't fortunate enough to receive an identity change. You know, that is the vast majority of their clientele, women released back into the world after two months. This identity alteration involved only six women. I have lots of questions, so yes, I'd like to go and get some answers."

After dinner, we took Tip for a long walk. We routed ourselves around the lake rather than along the main roads. It was dark early, so flashlights were a must. We admired the lighthouse, which sat at the end of a narrow peninsula jutting into the middle of the lake. We made small talk, trying to avoid the subject of abused women. I pondered why it was that the women who were the abused had to retreat to shelters and temporary homes like Mourning Doves with no money and little or no skills, in most cases. What about the abusers? Were they being treated? And if so, by whom? Or were they left alone to create their own personal hells for their families, unchecked by anyone? Did they go to counseling? Why weren't they in jail? Or were they? Seriously, I thought to myself. What about the men?

CHAPTER 32

BOARD MEETING

Wednesday brought three cases: two knee replacements and one hip replacement, all first timers.

One of the knee replacements was the husband of the day-shift head nurse at HCMC, Louann Simms. As is customary, I went out to the waiting room to let her know that Bob's surgery went just fine.

"Thanks, Dr. Brady. We're all so glad you're here. I know the drill about the post-op recovery, so don't waste your valuable time going over that with me. I did want to bring up the fact that you're going to have to send Bonnie McLellan home tomorrow. The utilization review nurse stopped by this morning and let me know. I know her situation is terrible, and her injury is equally as bad, but her diagnosis and treatment codes don't allow a longer stay. Otherwise, she might get stuck with a massive bill, and I doubt they can afford it."

"Do you know what her husband does for a living?"

"Waste management."

"You mean, like he owns a company?"

"No, sir, he works on a truck."

"You mean, a garbage truck?"

"Yes. You've heard of Big Tex Trucking Company? The waste management company is a subsidiary."

"I've heard that name in connection with the missing women. Someone worked for them."

"That's true. Margaret Harris was a dispatcher there, and Carla Robinson's husband was a driver for them."

"Huh. How do you know all that?"

"I read the papers, Doc, plus I've lived out here for twenty-five years."

"Anyway, Louann, Bonnie's husband is no spring chicken, and that's hard work, a job for younger and stronger men."

"He doesn't have any education, Dr. Brady. The company has excellent benefits, including health insurance and pension plans, so he's stayed with them all these years. You know, I've known them for a long time."

"No, I did not know that. So, you're aware of her . . . situation?"

"Yes, I am. That's why I hate to see her have to go home so soon. But we have no choice. We're all at the mercy of the insurance companies. I did put in a request for home health services. Hopefully her insurance company will approve that. At any rate, thanks for fixing up my hubby. I'll see you tomorrow."

After my surgeries were done, I stopped by and told Bonnie she would be leaving the next day. I decided she would be safer in a cast, so the nurses and I took her over to the cast room in a wheelchair, and I held the arm while the cast technician applied a plastic cast. At least it was her left arm. She could use her right hand for eating and cleaning herself . . . and defending herself, if my suspicions were correct.

The board meeting of Mourning Doves was held in the conference room that I met Buck Owens in when I first toured HCMC. Buck Owens and Sister Mads were, of course, present. Also present was Lynn Abbott, head of human resources for the hospital, Bill Porter, CEO of the hospital, Dr. Jackson Morse, chief of surgery, and Dr. Dan Burns, chief of anesthesia. I had met all four at that dinner they were having with Buck at the yacht club, back before we moved to the area. I introduced Mary Louise, since she had been in Houston when I had met the others. It seemed to me that there was a close, cozy relationship between the executives at HCMC and Mourning Doves. Perhaps that was due to the "transformation center," as I had come to think of it.

"We're waiting on two more. Please have a drink and an appetizer," said Buck.

There were sodas, water, coffee, and savory pastries. I didn't have to be asked twice to eat and drink. Mary Louise, of course, being her dainty self in a bold red pantsuit with matching red heels, sipped water and took tiny bites of a tart. Unlike me, she never had to worry about crumbs on her clothing.

The door opened and in walked two women. One I knew fairly well—Louann Simms, nursing supervisor of the day shift at HCMC. The other I did not know. She was tall with a dark complexion and a warm smile.

"This is Del Andersen," announced Buck. "She's the owner, publisher, and editor of the *Highlander*, the Highland Lakes local newspaper. She's a new addition to the board, as are Dr. Jim and Mary Louise Brady." We shook hands all around then sat and waited for Sister Mads to speak.

"We now have ten board members, five men and five women. Between the ten of us, there is a vast amount of experience in dealing with all kinds of people. We have Buck, former family doc, now oilman and chairman of the board of HCMC. We have Bill Porter, our CEO of HCMC. We have three practicing docs: Dr. Jim Brady, a new addition to the orthopedic surgery staff; Dr. Jackson Morse, chief of surgery; and Dr. Dan Burns, chief of anesthesiology. We have five women: me, a former nun and the director of Mourning Doves. We have Mary Louise Brady, a well-known Houston fundraiser; Lynn Abbott, head of HR here at HCMC; Louann Simms, a head nurse; and Del Andersen, a newspaper woman.

"We ten will be the continuing backbone and caretakers of Mourning Doves. This is a charity, but much more—so much more—than just a charity. We take in the abused, the downtrodden, the weak, the distraught, the helpless, and bring them up to a level of life they do not know. Independence. Strength. Fearlessness. Warriors for the cause of abused women everywhere.

"For those of you new to the board, I started Mourning Doves almost five years ago. I knew from previous experience with a shelter I set up within the auspices of the Catholic Church that you cannot help everyone. The shelter I established in Austin took all comers, day and night. We would get women with their children, sometimes babies, running from abusers, trying to get help, or even just a decent meal and a solid night's sleep. Our success rate was poor. Piss poor, excuse my French. We would house and shelter them for a few days, then they would return to their previous situation. And return again and again, same old song with unlimited verses.

"Buck and I have been friends for years through his efforts to rescue a niece from an abusive, intolerable situation. He told me of his plans to build a medical center in our area that would rival facilities anywhere in Texas. We eventually concocted this idea to join forces, to create an institution that not only would be friendly toward abused women but would have the facilities to actually transform a woman into someone else. Our goals were not unlike the witness protection program run by the US Marshals Service. I thought that if the federal government can handle identity changes, why couldn't a handful of smart folks with money do the same thing?

"Buck and I had many meetings about the procedures and protocols. He wanted to develop a separate private area in the hospital to go about making the changes we had discussed only theoretically, but with private investors and state and federal funds involved, we decided to hold off on that aspect of our plan. We have architectural diagrams of what that facility should look like, but it's still on the drawing board. We decided it best to send makeover specialists to Mourning Doves to make changes in the women's hairstyle, hair color, and makeup, and apply permanent eyebrows and eyeliner, items of a cosmetic nature but which produce a totally different look. We would then arrange for cosmetic surgery alterations to be done here at the hospital, during routine operating times, for facelifts, eyelifts, nose jobs, dental work, and underbite and overbite repair. The differences in pre- and post-alterations of minor aspects of a woman's face were remarkable. They became unrecognizable in most cases.

"Buck and I decided to take six women, all married but able to support themselves financially if necessary, all subjected to years of abuse, and give them the full physical makeover. We thought that having a woman disappear every other month would create a stir, but only briefly. Without any evidence of foul play, we figured the authorities would soon let the issue slide and we could breathe easily knowing our new creations were safely in place, especially since we would have signed agreements with the husbands to not investigate. And we would have been right, had it not been for that journalism grad student in Austin who wrote a piece about these women, which fell into the hands of our 'Curious George,' Dr. Jim Brady.

"However, as it stands now, we have six women in six new lives, away from their abusive home environments, virtually unknown to their former assailants, and we feel our efforts have paid off. Specifics about these women is limited to four people: Dr. and Mrs. Brady, who have only the women's biographical information prior to their change, and Buck and I, who have, in addition, their current locations, their workplaces, home addresses and contact numbers. Our fear has been that if this information came into the hands of their husbands and former abusers, the women would be at risk, even with the agreements; to what extent, we don't know. Would they aggressively pursue their wives? Would they try and kill them? Would they make nice and pretend to have changed and beg them to return, only to start the abuse all over again? We don't know and don't want to find out. Even their children only know that they are safe."

"The purpose of the board," Buck said, "is to find new ways to earn money in order to support the charity. We have to be very careful with the fundraising due to IRS laws about deductibility. If an individual donates say, $1,000 to Mourning Doves, the entire amount is deductible unless goods and/or services are provided in exchange for the donation. That amount has to be subtracted from the donation, and the patron is left with, for example, a $500 donation if they attend a party where drinks and dinner are served. We want to try and avoid that. We want straight donations with no goods or services provided. If donor money comes from a foundation, it's illegal to accept goods or services in exchange for the donation, and we want to keep foundation money completely deductible.

"In time, we would like to build our dream facility within the confines of the hospital, and we have plenty of room for it. But for now, we'll continue with cosmetic surgery done as needed through normal hospital channels, and cosmetology done at the Mourning Doves facility."

"I have a question for either one of you," said Mary Louise. "I realize the work you're doing and its value. And for the six women who were selected to disappear from their former lives, I'm certain you will have their eternal gratitude. But what about those left behind? When I worked the hotline in Houston, I felt like I was spinning my wheels. Abused women and children came in and out of women's centers like a sieve. I couldn't get a grasp if we were helping those women or not. I mean, sure we protected them for a night or two, but long-term? There was little training or education there, mostly just protected housing for a brief time.

"So, what are your statistics on the other women that have passed through Mourning Doves? The majority have stayed two months, been counseled and given medical, legal, and financial help, and as best as I understand the program, were then released back into their old situation, with expectations that things would be better for them. But I'd like to point out, while your participants have gained new skills, and their attitudes improved, and maybe even their strength of character improved, what about their abusers? Are they any different as a result of their so-called loved one's two-month absence? Are they going to suddenly play nice and be good spouses and partners? Have their attitudes changed? I've read statistics that show an abused woman's greatest chance to be murdered is when they are leaving or when they are returning to their abusive situation."

The room was very quiet. Neither Buck nor Mads said anything.

Then Del Andersen spoke up. "I agree with Mary Louise. I've worked the Austin-area women's centers off and on for years. You can protect a woman only when she's in your care. When she's back out in the world, she's at the mercy of her abuser.

"I'm happy to be on this board, and I, like probably the rest of you here, have seen the plans for a dedicated women's transformational area, and have visited Mourning Doves, and appreciate the work both Buck and Sister Mads have done. And I admire your tireless efforts to bring help to all the women in need, which are legion. And I'm happy to help raise money for a wonderful cause. But unless a woman has the educational and financial capability to stand on her own and go through the identity transformation, what are the actual rates of improvement among the rest of the women that pass through the facilities? How are we really doing in providing long-term help to these poor women?"

The conference room was again silent, when the door burst open. A man in a gray security services uniform was holding a bloody towel to his head.

"Dr. Owens, a man dressed in black came through the front sliding door and approached me for directions to a patient's room in the hospital, and when I turned and looked at the computer screen, he clubbed me. I think I passed out for a minute, and when I woke up, I saw your office door open. I ran in there, thinking you might be injured, but all I saw was your safe door open."

We all stood and followed Buck into his office. "Oh my God," he said, "all the identity papers on our transformed women are gone. How in the world . . .? Shit! I gave Lucy the combination in case something happened to me. Call the police and have them get to her house right away. Our escapees are in trouble. I've got to get to the bank and open my safe deposit box. I've got their info there as well. I have to get my banker on the phone!"

I saw cell phones being used and assumed that the local authorities would be dispatched to Lucy Williams's house and to HCMC forthwith. Mary Louise and I ran into the lobby, realizing this was an emergency. The new identities of the six women were in the hands of someone who was willing to kill for the information. I didn't know if these women were in state or out of state, but I knew one person that could help. Susan Beeson, the new ASAC for the FBI in Austin, had jurisdiction. She could mobilize the troops. Hopefully it wouldn't be too late.

CHAPTER 33

THE WOMEN

"**C**ome with me," Buck instructed to Mary Louise and me. We climbed into his black Suburban and drove to the Horseshoe Bay Trust. His banker was already there. There was no time for introductions. Buck produced his matching key for his safe deposit box, opened it, and grasped the stack of records. He thanked and shook the hand of his efficient trust officer and headed back to the SUV.

"We're going to Lucy's house, make sure she's okay."

"I called a friend of ours, Susan Beeson. She's the new ASAC for the FBI in Austin. She's just arrived, but she's the former chief of police in Houston and very capable. I've asked her to mobilize her forces, once I can see the names and locations of the women in question. Do you have a problem with that, Buck?"

"No, of course not," he said, speeding down FM 2147 and ignoring the 45-mile-per-hour speed limit. He had a police band radio, turned it to a specific channel, and broadcast that he was on an emergency mission and that no cops were to stop and harass him or he'd make sure all the police chiefs and sheriffs in the area would have their respective asses in the morning.

Mary Louise and I started looking through the files. We scanned them first, to get our bearings. The women were listed in alphabetical order of their real names, with their assumed identities in parentheses. They were all in Texas, which was a blessing. Susan Beeson would either have jurisdiction, or she could speak to the ASACs in Houston, Dallas, and San Antonio to help locate women in their districts. Each had a current address, place of employment, and cell phone number.

I called Susan and put her on speaker phone.

"Have you decided on a course of action?"

"Yes. What a disaster. I'll get my people on it right away. I think the easiest way to handle it is to tell them the truth. That their identities have been compromised, and that they need to get out of their houses ASAP. We don't know what kind of time frame we're looking at between the time the perp got the data on the women's whereabouts and how long it would take for him to reach each individual woman. I don't know if he's working alone, or with one or more other persons. I think it's best to notify all now. Do you have their contact info?"

"Yes, here goes:

"Hilary Allen, now Helen Hunter. Austin. Previous banker, same job at Frost Bank. 737-555-1130.

"Margaret Harris, now Peggy Jarvis. Austin. Previously a dispatcher, works in retail at Barton Creek mall. She's the one I recognized at Chico's in the Galleria mall. 737-555-1271.

"Carla Robinson, now Robin Charles. San Antonio. Previous nurse, same at University Hospital. 737-555-4644.

"Katie Smith, now Charlese Tryon. Dallas. Former event planner, now same at the Omni. She's the one whose daughter I spoke to. 512-555-9091.

"Karen Statton, now Cynthia Smith. Houston. Former nurse, same at Methodist Hospital. 737-555-4963.

"Jorja Watson, now Georgine Frick. Dallas. Former real estate broker, now works for RE/MAX. 512-555-7387."

"They all have emergency bags prepared," interjected Buck. "When we placed each woman with a new identity, we gave them specific instructions to keep a bag packed with items they would need for two or three days in case a disaster like this happened. Each should have cash, toilet articles, and a change or two of clothes ready to go. What are you going to tell them to do, Susan?"

"Go to a hotel far away from where they are living and wait for instructions from me."

"I guess that's best, although I can't imagine any way that whoever stole those files could get to one of women that fast, unless the women are in Austin," Buck responded. "Remind me which ones are in Austin, Jim?"

"There are only two in Austin, the former banker Hilary Allen with a lawyer husband, and the former Margaret Harris, former dispatcher now in retail, with a—oh shit—her husband is a Granite Falls detective. I don't know the man, but my advice, Susan, is to contact her first. Austin's only an hour away this time of night, and in a police car, who knows."

"I'll get right on it."

"Keep us posted, please."

Susan disconnected as we pulled in front of Lucy Williams's house. There were several neighbors standing in their yards or in the street. There was a black-and-white in the driveway with its roof lights on and siren off. We ran into the house and found two officers attending Lucy, who was on the floor of a small living room. She had taken a beating around the face and head and appeared to have a broken nose and a busted lip, and her left eye was swollen shut. There was blood coming from her right hand, and I saw that her little finger had been snapped off. She was minimally responsive.

"We've called the EMTs, they'll be here in five. Lady took a beating, man," one of the first responders said. "And that finger. What the hell did he want? Doesn't look like she had any money."

"Information," Buck said. "This is all my fault. Me and my fucking ego, trying arrogantly to save the world. What bullshit."

"Buck, who knew that Lucy had the code to your safe? And who would know that the dossiers on these missing women would be in that safe?"

"I don't know, Jim. She knew how valuable the documents in my safe were, and I can't imagine she would have told anyone about them. Seeing her now, having been tortured, she probably did give up the number to her attacker, since there is no other way my safe could have been opened."

We heard the ambulance arrive. The EMTs checked Lucy's vital signs, started an intravenous line, applied a blood pressure cuff, loaded her onto a gurney, took her to the ambulance, and departed, sirens wailing.

"I can't possibly forgive myself if something happens to Lucy. She lost a daughter, probably to her abusive husband, although it can't be proved. Now this. I'd like to blame her son-in-law for her injuries, but unless the crime-scene folks find something here or on her person at the hospital, that will probably be another dead end."

"We've called the crime scene investigators, and they're on their way," said one of the officers in attendance. "I told them the lady was in bad shape, and we had to send her with the EMTs. If there is any evidence on her personage, it may be lost in the emergency room. Sorry about that, but saving her life was the most important issue."

"No problem," said Buck. "You did the right thing. Do you need me for anything else?"

"No, sir."

We three returned to Buck's Suburban and sat there for a moment to gather our thoughts.

"What should we do?" asked Buck.

"Well, we can all go home and sit and wait to hear from Susan," responded Mary Louise. "She's the professional, she has the staff, she can probably get people to each of the Austin women's housing within the hour. That would be the prudent, logical, and sensible course to take."

"Jim?"

"I'm in the mood to pull someone's eyeballs out with a pair of pliers, so I vote we tear our asses to Austin and make sure Margaret and Hilary are safe. I'd love to back up the FBI."

"I'm with you, Jim. I can't just sit here and wait to see what happens. This is all my fault. I've got to try and make it right. Mary Louise?"

"Good, I was hoping you boys would say that. I needed to be the voice of reason, but since it's a two to one vote, I'm all in. Jim, I'll call our housekeeper, see if she can go sit with Tip until we get home. Okay?"

"Everything you say and do is better than okay."

Buck drove through some side streets, wound his way back to Highway 281, and headed south. He again got on his police radio, gave his location and destination, and requested a clear and unobstructed path to Austin on the state highways.

"It occurs to me that if Margaret Harris's husband, a Granite Falls detective, or Rob Bates, a deputy sheriff of Kingsland County, were involved in this mayhem, we might have trouble getting to our destination, Buck."

"Well, Jim, there are mostly good cops out there who know what we're up to and where we're headed. If those two men are involved, they would be outnumbered severely, so I think we're good with the plan. My worry is that if they are mixed up in this mess, they have a head start on us. Although I don't see why Bates would be involved in making his way to Austin. I can certainly see him as torturing his mother-in-law for my safe code because he's such a vindictive SOB, but once he had that information, seems to me his role in this fiasco would be done. I mean, his wife is dead."

"He could be helping the Granite Falls cop, though. He might have gone to the hospital, slugged the security guard, and robbed your safe. Or he might have had an accomplice that he radioed the safe code to who was already standing by at the hospital, and that person knocked out the guard. And Harris, the Granite Falls cop, could be the third accomplice and was on the road to Austin once his accomplices relayed the information about the current location of his wife. And maybe the lawyer, Hilary's husband, who lives in Austin, is involved, and he was standing by to receive the current location of his wife. If that's the case, we're seriously behind."

We sped south down Highway 281, then went east on Highway 71 toward Austin. Buck was doing 100 miles per hour, so it would be a short drive to the outskirts of the city. Then we would have to contend with the infamous Austin traffic, even though by then it was near ten o'clock.

Mary Louise's cell phone rang. She nodded her head, said okay. "That was Susan. She can't get hold of either woman. Their cell phones go immediately to voice mail. She has a couple of agents on the way, but there was a delay in getting hold of them."

"Shit. Tell me where we're going," said Buck. "And let's go to the cop's wife's home first."

"Let's see, she lives in West Lake Hills on Wildcat Hollow," I said. "Looks like the house is not far from the mall where she works. I don't mean to be critical, but Margaret Harris, now Peggy

Jarvis, is living in the same town as her husband, the attorney. I mean, seriously? Why not Dallas, Houston, or San Antonio? Or Boston, for God's sake?"

Buck punched the address into his navigation system. It was about twenty minutes away. Fortunately, traffic was clear.

"That was always an issue with relocation. We let the women choose where they wanted to go, and they often made choices in order to be close to a loved one, in case they were able to reunite. As I remember, Margaret has a mother in Austin and wanted to be able to check on her. Whether she exposed her real identity to her mother or not, I don't know. But I agree, decisions like that were not smart."

The GPS took us down Bee Caves Road, then left onto Westlake Drive, and another left onto Wildcat Hollow. It was a narrow road, secluded in a large forest. We turned down a tiny driveway and into a parking court. The house was a nice two-story. There were no lights on in the house. The front of the house was lit by small lamps on either side of the front door. Buck knocked and rang the doorbell, but there was no answer. We walked around to the back and saw a light on in what appeared to be the kitchen. We walked up three steps onto a porch, looked through a glass panel in the rear door, and saw nothing.

When we came back around to the front, a dark sedan was pulling in behind Buck's car. Two men stepped out of the car, one from each side of the front seat, drew their weapons, and flashed their FBI badges.

"Down on the ground! Now!" they yelled.

We did as per their instructions and attempted to show them some ID. Buck eventually was able to explain who we were after we were frisked. Mary Louise gave them Susan's cell phone number, which one of the agents called, and finally they were convinced we were part of the good guys' team and let us up from the ground.

"See anything?" one agent asked.

"Nothing," Buck answered. "We walked around to the back. There's a light on in the kitchen, but we didn't see anyone."

"Did you try opening the door?"

"No, but no one answered the doorbell or the knock," Buck said.

"Stay here, just in case," said the driver of the FBI vehicle to his partner. He then walked up to the front porch, turned the knob, and opened the front door. He pulled a small but powerful flashlight from his pants pocket and entered. The door opened into a small foyer, which led into a great room. We followed him as he explored the downstairs. We went through the kitchen, a master bedroom and bath, and a study/library. There was a stairway adjacent to the kitchen leading up, so we trailed behind the agent and went to the second floor.

There were two bedrooms with an adjoining bath between. We found Margaret Harris/Peggy Jarvis on the floor of the second bedroom. She was on her stomach, laying in a pool of blood from a gunshot to the back of the head. She was nude from the waist down. "Don't touch anything," the agent said. "Slowly back out of the room and go downstairs and wait." He used his wrist microphone to call his partner and told him to call in the local police to work a murder scene.

Once downstairs, we went outside and leaned against Buck's SUV. Buck held his head in his hands and literally sobbed. I heard him say, "All that hope, all that work, all that money, all that time, a great sacrifice for all concerned, and this is how it ends? Just like it would have, had we not made the effort. It was all a waste."

Mary Louise went over to Buck and tried to comfort him, but to no avail. "Buck, we still have the other woman. Hilary? There is hope for her. I'll call Susan and see if she's been located."

Mary Louise walked a few feet away. I followed and longed for a cigarette. I listened while she spoke to Susan. Fortunately, Hilary Allen/Helen Hunter had been found. She was late getting home from a social function her bank was hosting, and her cell phone had run out of juice. She didn't get Susan's call, so she had no idea that her identity had been compromised. Fortunately, by the time she arrived home, two FBI agents were already waiting outside her front door. They told her what had happened, followed her into the house so she could safely pick up her getaway bag, and took her to a hotel on the north side of Austin to await further instructions from Susan Beeson.

Mary Louise went back inside and told Buck that Hilary/Helen was safe. Upon hearing that news, he cried even harder.

CHAPTER 34

AFTERMATH

I was thankful that Thursday was a patient day, starting at nine o'clock in the morning. We hadn't made it back home until after midnight. Tip was a happy boy, although he'd been asleep, to which he returned after an appropriate greeting. We told Tonya to stay in the guest room and not try and get home that late.

I arrived at the hospital at eight o'clock, had some breakfast, signed some operative reports and other documents on my desk, and trudged through the day. I saw fifteen or twenty patients, a mix of new patients, follow-ups from surgery, and folks in for a second consultation after their MRI or CT scans were completed. I finished up a little after two o'clock and ate half a sandwich that Nurse Shelly provided from the kitchen.

I dictated the office visits into the magic machine that transformed my words into print data for the computer. I watched the computer screen to make sure the words being transcribed were what I actually said. One had to speak very distinctly, or some sort of gobbledygook would appear. The week prior, I was dictating notes about a patient who had a previous fractured knee, and the computer typed something about franks and beans. Weird.

I made rounds after clinic and made a point to stop by and check on Lucy Williams. Her little finger could not be salvaged, so the surgeon cleaned up the amputation and closed the wound. She did have a nasal fracture, and that had been set and splinted during the hand operation. She had sutures in her lip and bruises all over her face, and her left eye was still swollen shut. She was aware of my presence, as she reached out and grabbed my hand. Her right eye was watering, probably tearing, so I took a bedside tissue and gently wiped her eye and face.

"It was him, Dr. Brady, it was Rob. He had on a mask and hat and was in all black, but I could smell him," she rasped. "He always had this odd smell, like tobacco and onions. I admit I couldn't see his face, but it was him."

"Have the police been here?" I asked.

"Yes, but I was too groggy to respond coherently. I hope they return so I can tell them it was Rob that beat me up. He cut my little finger off with a pair of shears, told me he would cut them all off unless I told him Dr. Owens's safe code."

"We figured that's what he wanted. How in the world would he know you had that code?"

She turned her head away. "I had a log of all the times he beat me or Julie. I had photos of both of us after all our attacks. There was enough in that file to put the bastard away for life. He knew I had it, because I had threatened him with it many times. That's the only thing hanging over his head that kept him from killing us. And he knew it was in Dr. Owens's safe. I didn't tell him as much, but I always told him I had the dirt on him and it was in a safe place. I think he figured it out eventually. He's not stupid, just a monster."

"You get some rest, Lucy. I'll check on you tomorrow," I said, and headed for home.

Mary Louise constructed me a large Tito's vodka martini, very dirty, with plain olives. We sat on the terrace together as she sipped her Rombauer chardonnay and I decompressed while Tip held his fat head in my lap so I couldn't leave.

"To keep you informed and in the loop on the board activities, let me tell you what has happened today thus far. The Austin paper somehow obtained a photograph of the woman who was murdered last night. It was a morgue photo or a coroner's-office photo, and the quality was poor. You and I were there, so of course we know it's Margaret Harris a.k.a. Peggy Jarvis. Some enterprising reporter dug up the stories from the past year of the six missing women in the Highland Lakes area and postulated that perhaps this Peggy Jarvis murder was related in some way to those disappearances.

"Later in the day, the paper gets two phone calls telling them that the person identified as Peggy Jarvis looks a lot like a friend of theirs by the name of Margaret Harris, who disappeared two years ago and who used to work as a dispatcher at Big Tex Trucking Company. Next thing that happens is the television stations get hold of the story, and some reporter gets a photo of Margaret Harris from Big Tex. The TV station then displays photos of Margaret Harris and the deceased Peggy Jarvis side by side, and remarkably, despite some changes perhaps through plastic surgery, and the poor quality of the coroner's photo, they are determined by the reporter to possibly be the same person.

"To make matters worse, the crime scene technicians went over her house in great detail and found a travel bag. In the bag was a Ziploc plastic bag with cash and a credit card in the name of Peggy Jarvis, along with two changes of clothes and cosmetics. Unfortunately, there was another Ziploc plastic bag in the travel bag that had a driver's license and a credit card in the name of Margaret Harris. The driver's license photos of Peggy Jarvis and Margaret Harris were vaguely similar. Also, there were two emergency contact numbers in what the reporters are now calling a getaway bag. Would you like to know whose names were in there?"

"Do I have a choice?"

"No. Sister Madeline O'Rourke and Dr. Buck Owens. And it didn't take them long to discover that Buck is chairman of the board of HCMC, and that Sister Mads is the founder of Mourning Doves, and what that facility is for."

"Don't tell me that the reporters are now going after Mads and Buck?"

"Oh, yes, apparently it's been a zoo at Mourning Doves and HCMC. There have already been two reports of newspaper or television people falling into Lake LBJ trying to get around that eight-foot wall and access the house."

"Did you talk to Susan and find out about the other four women?"

"Yes. All four received her phone message, grabbed their emergency bags, and got out of their houses. Susan has them parked in a hotel along with Hilary Allen a.k.a. Helen Hunter."

"Is it safe to keep the five women in the same location?"

"She had limited agents available, so she did the best she could. She got three adjoining rooms with two queen beds each and has two agents per shift round the clock to make certain no harm comes to them. How long she will keep this up, I don't know.

"Listen, Jim Bob, this is mostly out of our civilian hands now. The murder of Margaret Harris/Peggy Jarvis is a local case, but because a violent crime occurred, there is a precedent for the FBI to get involved. Susan also thinks that because this murder is tied to a missing persons case that the FBI investigated last year, there will be no problem having the feds involved. At least that's her opinion as of this morning. Especially considering she now has five women parked in a hotel with new identities provided for by a local charity because of extreme spousal abuse, and allegedly funded through the Hill Country Medical Center courtesy of Dr. Buck Owens."

"That's kind of a quantum leap in judgment, isn't it? How can she say that without knowing what's really going on?"

"Jim Bob, that IS what's been going on. Maybe not the funding part by HCMC, but who knows. There certainly has been involvement of the institution via Buck Owens in order to keep Mourning Doves in business. Susan suspects there will be state and federal accountants over there tomorrow."

"My God, Mary Louise. All that work and strategizing to protect these battered women and it all comes down to this? Hell, Mourning Doves may well get shut down. How will that do any good for anyone? Sister Mads and her charity are going to be punished for trying to better the lives of abused women? What they have done is nothing more than an act of mercy."

"I don't disagree with you, but if you look at the situation from the outside looking in, I can understand how the press and TV people could jump to conclusions in order to make a better story. And you know as well as I do that while Buck and Mads and Mourning Doves may be front page news for a while, if these accusations don't pan out, the retractions will be on the back page. By the way, did you see Lucy today?"

"I did. The surgeon couldn't save the finger, so he completed the amputation. The ENT doc set and splinted her broken nose and stitched up her lip during the procedure on her hand. She has multiple bruises and a left eye that's swollen shut, but she'll recover from the injuries. She did tell me something interesting. She claims she knows it was Rob Bates that beat her up to get the code to Buck's safe. She didn't see him because of a mask and hat, but she smelled him."

"What?"

"She smelled him. She said he always smells like tobacco and onions."

"I wonder how much traction that will hold with the police. By the way, which police department is handling that investigation?"

"She called Granite Falls PD. She lives inside the city limits of Granite Falls."

"Hmm. Do you remember that Margaret Harris's husband was a cop?"

"Yes. I'd have to check but I think Granite Falls."

"Think they know each other, he and Deputy Sheriff Rob Bates?"

CHAPTER 35

ANOTHER FUNERAL

Margaret Harris's body was returned to her hometown of Granite Falls. The funeral was held Saturday in the First Lutheran Church. The proceedings were not open to the general public for obvious reasons, but the print and television media were there in droves. While neither Mary Louise nor I knew Margaret personally, we felt as though we were close to her as a result of her travails in escaping her abusive husband, Detective Randall Harris. She had no children but was close to a sister who lived in Austin, probably the reason Margaret selected that city to reside in when her identity changed. Both women had been raised in Granite Falls, and the sister, Olivia Munoz, decided the service should be held there.

Buck Owens and Sister Mads were in attendance and, because of our efforts in locating Margaret, albeit too late, had insisted we attend. The church was small, and the casket was closed. The gun she was shot with was a Glock 22 per Dr. Jerry Reed, the coroner and pathologist at HCMC. I had called him yesterday and asked him if he would mind if I attended the autopsy. We had met at Julie Bates's autopsy. The entry wound was from the rear of the skull, the occiput, and essentially blew off her face, thus the closed casket. Many people own Glocks, but it is currently the most common weapon used by law enforcement. She had suffered an assault prior to being shot, according to Dr. Reed. When we found her, she was nude from the waist down. There was no evidence of sexual activity, but he said there was severe trauma to the anus and vagina. He would have to perform further testing to elaborate on the subject, but that was all the information I needed. She died from a gunshot wound to the head, plain and simple, and was tortured before or after death by her assailant.

As was the case at Julie Bates's funeral, the law-enforcement husband Detective Harris showed up with a few colleagues, each wearing a shoulder patch from Granite Falls Police Department. I scanned the officers for shoulder identification from other police departments in the area, but there were none. Harris was a medium-sized man, not tall and not short, and thin. He was handsome in his uniform and cast an officious presence. He did not have the entourage that Deputy Sheriff Rob Bates's showed up with at his wife's funeral. Perhaps wife beating and murder were taking their toll on law enforcement in the area.

I had spoken to ASAC Susan Beeson about the investigation of Det. Harris with respect to his wife's murder. He was off duty that night and therefore used his personal vehicle, not the city sedan he used for his detective duties. She and her people were unable to confirm his presence in the area of the murder. There was no GPS evidence from his navigation system showing him there, nor did road-camera tracking between Granite Falls and Austin confirm his license plate. If he was in Austin and had killed his wife, he was a ghost.

Just as the minister had arisen from his chair in the pulpit area, the door to the church swung open. The cacophony of voices from outside the church disturbed the moment of silence. Five women marched down the center aisle of the church, flanked by men in suits, and with Susan Beeson in the rear of the procession. I knew these women from having studied their photographs many times. Katie Smith, Carla Robinson, Karen Statton, Jorja Watson, Hilary Allen. They marched to the coffin, bowed their heads, some nodded, some made the sign of the cross, all wept. They stood there for a moment, paying their respects, then turned and stared at the squadron of police officers supporting Det. Harris. With somber faces, they then sat together in the opposite-side front row. It was a moment of solidarity, and if there was any doubt that these five women somehow knew each other, and had bonded, and had lost a companion, that doubt was history. The six women who had disappeared together were compatriots, to be sure. They had lost one of their own, and they were here to let the world know that they were in this together, alive or dead, injured or whole, survivors or not. I felt the tide had turned within them. These women were different, changed somehow, through Sister Mads's program, and through their own increased strength and resolve, they were sending a clear message. DO NOT FUCK WITH US ANY LONGER. Their presence sent a cold chill down my spine.

The unspoken attitude in the press and television media changed. Once the five formerly missing women appeared at Margaret Harris's funeral, some of the leading women in the area as well as across the United States who were involved in women's shelters and in the treatment and care of the battered and abused stepped up to the plate. When they learned the stories of these women who had given up everything to flee their attackers, the shit hit the proverbial fan. Suddenly, the five surviving women were heroes, and deserved privacy, and admiration, and Austin and the Lakes area was invaded by civil rights lawyers and protestors of all sorts, demanding justice for these women.

Part of the reason for the uprising was that the women being housed by ASAC Susan Beeson at an undisclosed hotel were going to be charged with a crime: using fake IDs. Here they were, victims of abusive husbands, who had chosen to change their lives and get new identities to escape the inhumanity of their existence, only to be charged with a crime that had no victim.

I read a good deal of the pundits' banter back and forth online. Seems it was okay to possess fake IDs, and even okay to CREATE fake IDs, but it wasn't okay to USE fake IDs. Penalties ranged from up to a year in prison and up to $10,000 in fines for misdemeanor possession, and up to ten years in prison and up to $100,000 in fines for felony possession. Confiscation and destruction of their picture identity cards was a guarantee. By the time these women were put through the ringer, everybody on the planet would know their real identity, the new identities gone with the wind. And what would they do then? Go back to their old jobs? Return to the abusing husband? Of course, with all the publicity, the abusers would have to be very careful for a while. But when the dust settled, and the next great news story happened, and the plight of these runaways forgotten, where would these women be? Would they be safe? I had doubted it until that day at the funeral. Now, I wasn't so sure. The look on the survivors' faces told a new story, an awakening, an eruption of strength, a changing of the guard. Abusers, run like hell, because we're coming after you.

I pondered these events at length and determined the whole scheme concocted by Sister Mads and Buck was flawed from the beginning and probably doomed to failure. Only the US Marshals Service had continuing and predictable success hiding people with new identities, and even being part of a large governmental agency didn't afford it total success in all cases. Creating new identities and having these women disappear was an idea born out of passion for a cause and was understandable in theory but, as it turns out, imperfect in its delivery. However, the point of it all had been made, and now the world could see these five surviving women and look to them to initiate a global change in attitude. WE DO NOT HAVE TO TAKE THIS SHIT ANY LONGER.

I had so many unanswered questions swimming around in my head. Why hadn't Randall Harris been arrested already? There were affidavits in Margaret's file that I had reviewed with Mary Louise and Susan where he admitted to abusing his wife. I thought that if it happened again, or if he tried to locate her, he would be on his way to jail. But that had not happened. And she was dead, murdered, and he was still working as a detective in the Granite Falls Police Department, as far as I knew.

And what about Big Tex Trucking? That name kept coming up in the mix. Margaret Harris had worked there as a dispatcher. Carla Robinson's husband was a long-haul driver for the company, and Seth McLellan was a driver of a waste truck owned by a subsidiary. Was this a coincidence? Just a large employer in a small town?

Buck called another board meeting for Monday. He wanted to discuss the fallout after the missing women had been acknowledged publicly, and what his and Sister Mads's plan was with regards to Mourning Doves. All ten members were present.

"I wanted us to get together and talk about what's happened and what our plan for the future is. As you probably have read in the paper or seen on television, I am publicly accused of mishandling revenues from HCMC and comingling them with donations to Mourning Doves to support the facility. This is ridiculous. I've had forensic accountants from every applicable federal, state, and local agency in my office since Thursday looking for evidence of misappropriation of funds from the hospital. They won't find anything because there is nothing to find. I spoke to the lead investigator this afternoon, and he feels like this will pass soon. They have found nothing. I made available my personal financial information for inspection, supervised by my personal accountant and attorney.

"I have donated a lot of money to Mourning Doves these past five years, and along with good generous friends of mine, we have kept the charity going. While we do ask the women who have been residents there for a monthly contribution of $200 once they get back on their feet, that isn't enough to keep the place afloat. If every former resident was able to pay that amount, we'd have over a million dollars of yearly revenue. But that isn't going to happen. It costs a couple of million dollars a year to feed, house, and provide counseling and support services to the residents, plus the additional makeover and surgical costs for those selected few. My friends and colleagues bought the land and built the house, so there is no debt on the property. But there are maintenance costs, taxes, insurance, and repair costs.

"Mads and I now realize, with the fallout from our failed identity changes, that a different course of action should have been taken. But it's too late to reverse all that. Mads will continue to run Mourning Doves and will continue all our programs, which are designed to rehabilitate our patients in an attempt to get their lives back on track. Mads?"

"I'm thinking of longer stays, allowing more time away from the home environment. I realize only Doc Brady and Mary Louise were at the funeral, but did you see the looks on those five women's faces when they walked down the aisle to the casket? And their expressions when they turned and stared at those police officers? If looks could kill, that Randall Harris would be a dead man. Those women were changed. Maybe it was the length of time

away from their abusers, some almost a year. Or maybe our programs provided a needed change in their lives. Or maybe it was
the physical change in their faces and new identities. Or maybe
some combination of all those factors. There will be no more identity changes, I can tell you that. So we'll concentrate on making
internal alterations in our residents. But I will never forget the
expressions on those five faces. That was worth all the heartaches
and pain."

Buck spoke up again. "I wanted to meet with you all to give
you an opportunity to resign from this board. I don't think any of
you will have any repercussions from the various investigations,
especially those of you who had just joined, like the Bradys and
Del Andersen. We made some mistakes, but our cause is just, and
essential. We're going to keep going with or without you, but
Mads and I hope it's with you. Thanks for coming. The meeting is
adjourned."

CHAPTER 36

SHERIFF HOLMES AND CHIEF FERTITTA

Life is more fun when you poke the snake. You might get bitten, you might die, but you won't be bored.

With that in mind, on a Friday afternoon after a splendid round of golf at Apple Rock, I made an unannounced visit to Sheriff Holmes at the Kingsland County Sheriff's Office. I went through the metal detector, and also got a pat down to make certain I wasn't carrying a weapon. The same grumpy officer was still maintaining the entry as before. He didn't ask for my ID, so I had to assume he remembered who I was.

"What do you want to see Sheriff Holmes about?"

"Personal business. I'll discuss it with him."

"That's not good enough. I need to know your business with him."

"No you don't. I live in Granite Falls, and the sheriff is an elected official, allegedly available to any voter in the county. My business is with him, and him only."

The deputy glared at me but turned and picked up a phone and spoke into it quietly. He hung up, turned back around, and told me to follow him. He escorted me into Sheriff Holmes's office.

The sheriff was already standing in front of his desk, arms folded across his chest, with an unpleasant look on his face.

"So, back again, Dr. Brady. What can I do for you on this fine Friday?"

"I won't bore you with all the details, but I'm sure you've been reading the newspapers and watching the news, so you are aware of the six local women who were abused by their husbands so severely over a long period of time that they took the huge risk of assuming new identities. Some of these husbands have been punished due to loss of employment and financial failure, others are going to jail due to affidavits that were under lock and key until Dr. Buck Owens's safe was broken into. But I'm sure as the sheriff of Kingsland County, you're well aware of what all has happened here, right under your nose."

"Now see here. You can't blame me for these events. None of my officers were involved. My boys have clean records."

"Wrong. Let's talk about Deputy Rob Bates."

"He hasn't been charged with a crime. His wife wasn't part of the six women that disappeared, anyway."

"I came to see you months ago and told you Bates was stalking me. I also told you that his wife Julie had confided in her mother and insisted that her husband had shoved her into that oncoming car at the theater and caused her injuries. You did nothing about that. I told you that Bates had entered his wife's room at HCMC in the early morning hours and pummeled her recently healed incision with his fists. And you did nothing about that. So fast forward a month, and Julie is found murdered in her mother's house, raped, leg broken below my hip prosthesis, by a man dressed in some sort of protective clothing who went to the trouble of using a condom and applying bleach to her perineal area to avoid detection. And that happened because you did nothing about Bates."

"There was no evidence that he was involved. I'm sorry for her murder, but that case is still open and active. We have no suspects."

"Oh, you have a suspect, you just refuse to see it that way. And let me add one more thing. On the night of the break-in at Dr. Owens's office, someone managed to torture Lucy Williams into giving up the safe code. Lucy said she didn't see the man's face, but she knew it was her former son-in-law because he smelled like tobacco and onions. And yet you stand there and tell me Rob Bates is an exemplary officer? That is beyond bullshit."

"I don't know anything about this smell thing. Tobacco and onions?"

"She gave that information to the Granite Falls police officers. You people don't share crime scene evidence with each other?"

"Of course we do, but that bit of information never made it to my desk."

"Do you see where I'm going with all this? Probably not, so I'll spell it out for you. You let Bates get by with shoving his wife into a moving vehicle. You let him get by with assaulting her in the hospital. As a result, you're directly responsible for allowing Julie Bates to be murdered, and if that wasn't enough, he almost killed Lucy Williams, extracting information from her. And if you add all that to Bates's pattern of spousal and mother-in-law abuse going back for years, you have a sadistic murderer on your hands, and you refuse to do anything about it. A fine example of law enforcement you are, sir."

"You've got no evidence!" he screamed. He looked like he was going to have a stroke.

"Tell you what, Sheriff. I'll add another tidbit to the criminal life history of Deputy Rob Bates. I suspect he was involved in the murder of Margaret Harris in Austin. I think he tortured Lucy Williams for the safe code, and once he had it, he called Det. Randall Harris, who was already in Austin, and gave him Margaret's address, allowing Harris to torture and kill his wife.

You might want to look into the backgrounds of Bates and Harris, see if their paths have crossed before. He's an abuser also, enough so that his wife risked everything to get a new identity. And where did she end up? Dead, just like Julie. I hope you're proud of yourself. What a fine job you've done of protecting and serving the residents of the Highland Lakes area.

"Have a great fucking day, Sheriff," I said, and stormed out of his office.

I was on a roll and didn't feel the need to stop. I drove directly to the Granite Falls Police Department, all the while checking my rearview mirror for Deputy Bates. I asked to see Chief Fertitta and was pleased to see that Sgt. McCready was still at the entry desk to the police station.

"Dr. Brady again? Still out trying to solve crimes?"

"Nope. I've solved them. I would like to share my findings with the police chief, because it seems to me you all need help doing your job."

He stared at me, then told me to have a seat and left the room. My cell phone buzzed. It was Mary Louise calling, so I answered.

"Where are you?" she asked.

"Running some errands. I won't be too long."

"Susan Beeson just called me. Seems she just received a call from the Granite Falls police chief, who told her you were sitting at the police station, expecting to talk with him."

Busted. "Yes, that's right. I had to get some things off my chest. I stopped and had a nice chat with Sheriff Holmes at Kingsland County first, and now I'm here waiting to talk to Chief Fertitta."

"Susan told me that he and her dad are old friends, so out of deference to that, he's going to speak with you. But then you need to come home. We've had this conversation many times, Jim. You're an orthopedic surgeon, not a private investigator, not an

FBI agent, not a police officer. You're a doctor with a fake badge who needs to let law enforcement do their job."

"And I would be happy to, if they would do it correctly. I'll see you soon."

Sgt. McCready returned and motioned me to follow him. I had to walk past some desks in open cubicles. I got a few malevolent stares and wondered if Randall Harris was present. I had only seen him the one time, at Margaret's funeral.

"Dr. Brady, good to see you again," Chief Fertitta said, shaking my hand. "What can I do for you today?"

"I'll get right to it, Chief. You have a detective on your staff by the name of Randall Harris. I'd like to—"

"Now before you get all wound up, Doc, you should know that Randall has come clean with me and the department. Before these affidavits came to light, showing Randall's previous admissions of guilt in abusing his wife, he was contrite. When his wife went missing, he started going to counseling. He was determined to change his ways, should she ever return. He was heartbroken and desperately wanted her back in his life. When she was found murdered in Austin, he was devastated. He had to take a leave of absence. He's only recently returned to work. I believe he is a changed man, Doctor, and a model citizen and police officer."

"Really. So you don't think he killed his wife?"

"What??? Of course not. There isn't any evidence to even suggest such a thing."

"Here's what I think, Chief. There is a link somewhere between Randall Harris and Rob Bates. Two officers of the law, living in the same area, both spousal abusers. I don't believe you wake up one morning and start beating on women. I think that's a pattern, established and developed for years, culminating in a horrible outcome for the unlucky women who happen to be there when spousal anger is at its zenith. Harris got by with abusing Margaret for years, as Bates did with Julie. I believe Rob Bates killed Julie in a fit of rage, and I believe Randall Harris killed Margaret in a state of anger that knew no bounds. She had embarrassed him by running away. He was exposed for what he really was by an affidavit, all of which he believed was his wife's fault, not his.

"I think that Bates had an inkling about the missing women, that perhaps they weren't running but were hiding and were supported in some way by Dr. Buck Owens and Sister Mads. Maybe Lucy had told Julie, maybe Julie hinted it somehow to Rob Bates by accident, or through torture. And I think Bates got in touch with Harris, told him that the women were all stashed somewhere, and that he figured that information was in the possession of Owens, probably in his office safe, which I'm sure he knew about. So they hatched a plan. Bates had already killed his wife Julie—and yes I know, there is no evidence—so he would torture the safe code out of Lucy Williams, open the box and get Margaret's current address and identity, and then Harris could make his way there and finish off his wife once and for all for all the pain and suffering she had caused him. And it had to be done quickly, before the authorities had a chance to mobilize the troops and rescue the women before something bad happened to them. I think Bates and Harris lucked out, with Margaret relocated to Austin. She was less than an hour away."

"Susan Beeson, your FBI friend, has been here, and we've looked over the evidence. Randall was off duty that night, driving his personal vehicle. We searched the cameras all along Highway 71 on the route to Austin, and cameras along Bee Caves Road, and his license plate number is not seen. We also checked the nav system in his vehicle, and there is no entry for the address in question on Wildcat Hollow. And Randall said he was nowhere near Austin that night, and we have no evidence to refute that. I'm sorry, Dr. Brady, but there's nothing we can do without proof."

He stood and again shook my hand, and I went home.

CHAPTER 37

WHERE ARE THEY NOW?

Weeks passed, and the furor died down, as Mary Louise predicted. The major newspapers in Austin, Dallas, Houston, and San Antonio gradually moved positive information about the players involved—Dr. Buck Owens and Sister Madeline O'Rourke—toward the back of the front section and eventually quit reporting on the issue completely. Only our local paper, the Highlander, owned and operated by Del Andersen, continued the reporting. I could tell she and Mary Louise were going to hit it off from the first time they met at the Mourning Doves board meeting. Del came up the ranks as a reporter and gradually assumed her role as editor, then owner of the Highlander. Mary Louise had gained success in the same fashion, working her way up from shop girl to retail executive.

I continued with my practice on a slower scale, although patients were coming in for surgical procedures in droves, and my worry was that I could not handle the volume. I didn't want to be back in the situation from whence I came—too busy to enjoy the work. I had seen Bonnie McLellan a few times. Her cast was off, and she was doing therapy to try and restore her finger motion. Her husband Seth seemed almost doting over his wife for a change. And Bonnie seemed to have some life to her again.

Hopefully something had come over both of them in a positive manner as a result of the goings-on in our little community.

Lucy Williams recovered from her finger amputation and her broken nose, and her eye had healed. She had diminished eyesight in the injured eye but could see well enough to return to work as Buck Owens's admin assistant. I had spoken to her several days before her return to work and she related that she had been to the sheriff's office in Kingsland County and had filed a complaint about her former son-in-law, Deputy Rob Bates. Sheriff Holmes, the man I'd met once in his office, was none too friendly to Lucy and laughed in her face when she told him that she was sure that Bates was her assailant because of the tobacco and onion smell. She was worried that she would never get justice for the murder of her daughter Julie, nor for herself, since there were no suspects and no concrete evidence for either crime. But she carried on.

I came home from work one Thursday evening, bone tired and in need of liquid refreshment. I heard laughing coming from the terrace, and I walked out to see Del and Mary Louise in stitches over something. Tip rose from between the two women, came over and accepted a good rub, then went back and laid down.

"Hey, Del, Mary Louise. What is so funny?"

"Oh, Jim Bob, some of the fallout from the solving of the disappearing women case is just too much. It has to do with the husbands mostly. Del has been telling me stories. She's in the know, you know," and they started up again with the cackling. "Fix yourself a drink and come sit and listen."

I did just that, in the mood for a Macallan twelve-year-old scotch. I returned outside and sat.

"So, Jim Bob, the big papers have quit reporting on the story of our women, returned from the dead, if you will. I, however, keep the banner flying for women overcoming spousal abuse through the *Highlander*. In my position, I get all sorts of information, not only from my reporters but from readers who call in, write, email, text, tweet, however they are comfortable sending me happenings on the parties involved. I was telling Mary Louise that while these remaining five women are not publicity hounds, and they try to avoid interviews where they have to show their faces, they are not beyond giving us stories about their lives before they went to Mourning Doves and had identity changes, and how things are going now that they have returned.

"You do know that two of the women have returned to their homes and families and jobs, don't you?"

"I believe I read that in the *Highlander*, yes. I remember thinking how incredibly awkward that had to be. I mean, an abusive husband, who has tortured his wife in the past, now facing a woman with a new attitude, someone he no longer knows."

"That's exactly right. And did you know that Dr. Buck Owens was forced to produce his dossier on each woman that he and Sister Mads helped to disappear? The dossier included not only their new identities, but documentation of previous injuries, trips to the emergency room, and operations that had to be performed as a result of their spouses' physical abuse. And now that these men have been under the microscope since their wives' return, all sorts of unpredictable happenings are going on.

"Let me give you an example. Katie Smith, fifty-two years old, vanished January 15. A year ago now. She worked as an event planner here at the Hill Country Resort. Her name change was Charlese Tryon, and she landed a job at the Omni in Dallas as an event planner, same position she had in her old life. Well, she's done well for herself. The Hill Country Resort hired her back, putting her in charge of ALL event planning, including weddings, and she is doing very well. She threw her dentist husband out, physically as I understand it, and the fall broke his right arm. Now that would be a problem for a right-handed dentist under normal circumstances, but it's not. Want to know why, Jim?"

"Certainly."

"Well, with all the newspaper articles and television shows depicting his abuse toward her, with details about her ER visits, including a broken ankle, two shoulder dislocations, a nasal fracture, and her D&C, during which she was discovered to be eight weeks pregnant from spousal rape, it seems that the formerly successful dentist has no patients. He had two offices, but closed the satellite office first due to lack of business, and now has closed the second office. He has declared bankruptcy and is living in his car. They both had signed the affidavit, so he's also facing jail time, the amount to be decided by the judge. Katie has filed for divorce. She's reunited with her two grown children. Her life has completely turned around for the better, and her ex-husband to be is up shitz creek without a paddle. You gotta love it."

"While I don't wish misfortune on anyone, I think no one deserves it more than the husbands of our missing six."

"Why do you say missing six? Margaret is dead."

"I'd really like to call it the missing seven, since Julie Bates was scheduled to be the next vanishing woman. You remember she was hit by a car exiting the movies and sustained a broken hip and pelvis, which is how I came to know her. The planned exit from her life at the time was postponed because of her injuries, and ultimately she was murdered as well. No one has been arrested for the crime, by the way. There are no suspects, according to her mother, although she is convinced that Rob Bates is the guilty party."

"Now I remember," said Del. "Maybe some evidence will turn up. It usually does, in time. Listen, I've got to run. I prepared pieces for the *Highlander* on all five returning women and, now that the dust has settled, where they are in the process of taking back their former lives. It will run in a few days, but I brought copies for you two to read. Thanks for the wine, Mary Louise."

They air-kissed, Del left, and I sat back down.

"Are you hungry?" Mary Louise asked.

"Starving."

"How about crab salad and clam chowder?"

"Where are we going?"

"Nowhere. I picked it up at the market today. Why don't you take a shower while I put dinner together? I have a bottle of Ridge chardonnay chilling in the freezer."

How could you not love a woman like that?

There is an old saying that seafood such as oysters with spicy sauce can trigger labor. I can't comment on that, but I can state with some assurance that spicy seafood causes extreme horniness.

"Wow. What's got into you, Jim Bob Brady? You're like a teenaged boy tonight."

"I don't know. Horseradish? Tomorrow is Friday and I get to go play golf at the Summit. That always puts me in a good mood."

"Well, whatever you got, bottle it up and save some for next time." With that, she turned over and went to sleep immediately.

I, however, was wired. I got out of bed, careful not to disturb her or the sleeping Tip, and went into the great room bar, poured myself a wee dram of thirty-year-old Macallan scotch, and sat and opened the file Del had left. She had already verbally summarized the current status of Katie Smith, so I skipped her and went to the next. Del had them arranged in order of disappearance.

Margaret Harris was the first to vanish and was thirty-seven years old at the time she disappeared. She was a dispatcher at Big Tex Trucking, but when she changed her name to Peggy Jarvis, she opted to go into the retail business. I had recognized her at Chico's in the Austin Galleria, but shortly thereafter she moved to a store in the Barton Creek mall. Her husband was Randall Harris, a Granite Falls detective. Her documented injuries related to spousal abuse were a concussion and a wrist fracture. The various affidavits were released after Margaret was murdered. Through some quirk of fate, Margaret's wasn't signed. Legal counsel for her husband argued that the affidavit wasn't legal if not signed, and therefore he not only walked away from a potential murder charge, he wouldn't serve time for his abusive behavior.

Carla Robinson was forty-four years old when she vanished two months after Margaret. Carla had been a nurse at Hill Country Medical Center. She changed her name to Robin Charles, moved to San Antonio, and had been hired as a nurse at University Hospital. Her husband was a long-haul trucker for Big Tex Trucking Company. Her documented past injuries had included fractured ribs with a punctured lung, and a laceration to the sole of the foot. She had moved back into the house she shared with her husband. She got her old job back at HCMC with a promotion to head nurse on the three-to-eleven shift. She and her husband had been going to counseling, but in reality, the fact that he was on the road a large part of the time gave them enough separation time to make the transition easier. She rescinded her affidavit, removing the option for her trucker husband to serve jail time for his actions toward her. Her only daughter graduated from college, disgusted with both her parents, and moved far away, hoping no one would recognize her last name.

I again pondered if there was some connection between Margaret Harris working as a dispatcher for Big Tex Trucking and Carla Robinson's husband working as a truck driver for the same company. And there was Seth McLellan, who worked as a waste truck driver in a subsidiary company. Coincidence? Probably. I would never know for sure. Little details of unanswered questions bother me. Always have, always will. Noah's boat survived the flood when it rained for forty days and forty nights. Jesus was tempted in the desert, again for forty days and forty nights. Moses wandered the desert with the Israelites for forty years. What's this with the number forty? My parents could not provide an answer. My college professors couldn't either. Accept it and move on, I was always told. Sorry, that didn't work for me back then, and it doesn't work for me now.

Karen Statton, forty-eight years old when she was the third woman to disappear, had changed her name to Cynthia Smith. She had been at nurse, also at HCMC, and took a similar position at Methodist Hospital in Houston. She wasn't fond of her husband, an engineer at the Ferguson power plant, when she lived with him prior to her disappearance, and she wasn't fond of him when she returned. Her knee still ached from the two patellar dislocations he had caused. She filed divorce papers, took her old name back, and remained in Houston. Her son had by then graduated medical school, and he chose an internship and residency in Houston to be close to his mother. Mr. Statton had been fired from his job. His current whereabouts were not known. He would not serve jail time if he couldn't be located.

Jorja Watson, thirty-nine, was the fourth woman to vanish. She had assumed the name Georgine Frick and taken a job in Dallas with RE/MAX, a large real estate company. She and her husband, he of the Q-tip eardrum-rupture fame, had owned Bay Country

Realty together. The business suffered after her disappearance, but sales really plummeted upon exposure of her husband as an abuser. The company had no listings whatsoever. Rather than try and rebuild the company, with or without her husband, she decided that she was still young, and having no children or other ties to the area, she remained in Dallas with REMAX. She filed for divorce, giving her ex-husband to be her half of the business, which by then was worthless. When asked by Del what she thought her ex-husband was going to do now, her answer was, "I don't know and I don't care." He would be serving jail time.

Hilary Allen was forty-six when she disappeared. She had been a banker in the Lake LBJ area and continued in that same role with Frost Bank in Austin as Helen Hunter. Her husband was still practicing law in Austin, although his reputation had suffered. However, he was a litigator, a plaintiff's lawyer in the business of suing hospitals, doctors, and insurance companies, and his services were always in demand. Hilary decided to stay in Austin. Her oldest was a lawyer now, practicing with a defense firm, her middle child was in law school, and her youngest, whom I had interviewed back when these women were believed to be missing, had gained a position at an Austin bank. I presumed he was content now. Hilary did not rekindle her relationship with her lawyer husband. They were Catholic and had not divorced but rather had chosen to live separate lives. Hilary had developed arthritis of the lower spine from her fractures sustained by an angry husband jumping up and down on her back. She required daily pain medication. Inexplicably, her children had convinced her to rescind the affidavit their father had signed as well, so Mr. Allen the lawyer could continue to sue whomever he pleased without interruption.

Five women returned, and only Katie Smith and Carla Robinson stayed in town. And only Carla Robinson had stayed with her husband, although that could be temporary. Two women had paid for their escape with their lives—Margaret Harris and Julie Bates. I looked through the files again to see if Det. Randall Harris had suffered any consequences, and I noted that he had not been charged with his wife's murder, for lack of evidence. Plus the affidavit had not been signed. He was free and clear, living his life without repercussions.

I also had to lump Deputy Rod Bates in with Harris. He had not been charged with a crime, neither for killing and raping his wife nor for his savage beating of Lucy Williams, not that anyone could prove it. The other husbands had suffered consequences for their actions, which didn't justify their previous behavior, but at least they had been punished.

I finished my scotch, poured another. What a nasty business this had been. It left a bad taste in my mouth. Imagine how the women who had experienced the trauma felt. I tried to put myself in their respective positions, but that was impossible. Buck and Mads had done some good work and would continue to do so, but at what price.

CHAPTER 38

BATES AND HARRIS

Mary Louise was standing on the front porch when I arrived in the front drive, one hand on her hip and the other on the doorframe. Tip sat next to her, ears perked. It was the perfect picture for a Hallmark card, when you cared enough to send the very best.

"My little detective, out stirring up the taxpayers' law enforcement teams. Both men you talked to called the feds, were directed to Susan Beeson, and, according to her, whined and complained about you like little boys on an elementary school playground."

"Good. Maybe they will get off their respective asses and find our who assaulted Lucy Williams and killed Julie Bates and Margaret Harris. Although I've already figured that out, as I told the chief and the sheriff, in no uncertain terms. Thing is, I can't prove it, and I'm afraid they can't either, which leaves all three cases open and unsolved. And I just can't stand that."

"We have a Mourning Doves board meeting tonight, so you better get going if you want to have dinner. Food at six, meeting at seven."

I patted Tip on his fat head and rubbed both ears, and he closed his eyes and relished in the attention. I went directly to the shower, cleaned up, and dressed in khakis and a sweater. The weather was beginning to warm, but it still became chilly once the sun set.

We drove to HCMC and parked in my personal parking space, which at one time sounded grand. But with two killers on the loose, both in law enforcement, I was at a disadvantage if they wanted to confront me. My name was right there on the sign. It would be goodbye Dr. Brady, and hello Jesus . . . I hoped.

"What's this meat?" I asked Mary Louise. We were in a short buffet line in a private space adjacent to the large conference room.

"Some kind of pork. Maybe pulled pork?"

"Looks like shredded something for sure. Think I'll have the chicken. That pork dish is just too ugly to eat." Mary Louise looked at me like I had lost my mind, which was entirely possible.

The meeting started promptly at seven. "There have been no resignations from the board," said Buck. "For that, Mads and I are grateful. We'd like to review our statistics from the last month or so. Mads?"

"As you all know, we're not a 'drop-in' facility. We are an end-stage, the-buck-stops-here facility. Women make an appointment to come, and they are selected by a long list of criteria. I would love to take all comers, but it's not possible. I've gone to a minimum three-month stay, which, as I discussed at the last meeting, seems to better cement what the women have learned. This reduces the number of women passing through the facility from 120 to 80 per year. I can only hope they will be able to transform themselves as well as our original six did, but only time will tell.

"We have learned one fact very important to this business we're in, and that is that strength in numbers matters greatly. I'll never forget the looks on those women's faces at Margaret Harris's funeral. They had bonded, and they were a team. We're emphasizing that now with our new residents.

"Our donations have tripled since we had all the . . . publicity. I believe we inadvertently opened the door to an increased national conversation about the problem of battered and abused women. Also, as a result of help from many of Buck's friends, our board's friends, and the state of Texas judges, all charges against the returning five for using false identities have been dropped. These women are now free and clear to resume their lives as they see fit."

We clapped in unison.

"Del wrote a nice treatise, published in the *Highlander*, entitled 'Where Are They Now?' Good job, Del, informative and enlightening.

"Lastly, my heart aches for the lost lives of Margaret Harris and Julie Bates, and for the brutal beating of Julie's mother Lucy. I call the sheriff's office at Kingsland County and the Granite Falls Police Department every week, demanding justice for these two fallen women. So far, nothing has been done and no one has been charged, due to a surprising lack of evidence. Usually there is something, a hair left behind, a fingerprint on a bullet, a dollop of DNA left behind somewhere, even a passerby who saw something. But there is no evidence in these cases to point to an assailant and murderer. The cops tell me they don't expect that to change and are prepared to put these cases in a cold-case file in another month. I wish we had a real live Harry Bosch on staff. We sure could use him."

A month later, I received a text on my phone from Del Andersen. It was early on a Monday morning, while I was having breakfast before my surgical cases. The text directed me to a website for the *Highlander* and read "you're going to want to see this article."

Two local law enforcement officers, Deputy Sheriff Rob Bates, and Granite Falls Detective Randall Harris, were found dead this past week under bizarre circumstances. This reporter has discovered they were friends in high school, having played football and graduating from Burnet High School the same year, and my assumption is they continued to be friends over the years. There were photos of them together in both their homes, on hunting and fishing trips.

Harris lived in an apartment on Lake LBJ in Granite Falls, and Bates lived on several acres of fertile land on the north side of Lake LBJ near Granite Shoals but in Kingsland County. Neither had shown up to work for the past several days and had not responded to phone calls. They were both found in a barn on Harris's property by the caretaker who mowed the property weekly. Each was tied with baling wire around their arms and legs to a vertical support beam in the barn. Their faces were bloody and disfigured, indicative of repeated beatings. Fingers and toes had been hacked off in an irregular fashion with some sort of dull instrument, and both had been castrated. Cause of death was attributed to blood loss from multiple sites.

The coroner told this reporter that it was apparent the victims had been tortured for at least a day, possibly two, but there were no clues at the scene as to why they were targeted. Both had been under investigation at one time for the murder of their wives, but there was no evidence and the cases went nowhere. Both were suspended for a time, then reinstated.

The coroner was puzzled that there was little or no evidence at the crime scene, no hair fibers other than that belonging to the victims, no DNA other than from the victims' blood, and no clues as to the identities of the assailant or assailants. He had assumed that with all the blood and gore, some sort of clues would have been obtained from the crime scene that would point law enforcement in the right direction to solve the crime. But that was not to be.

Anyone with information regarding this crime is directed to call either the Kingsland County Sheriff's Department, or the Granite Falls Police Department.

THE END

READ ON FOR A SNEAK PEEK
OF ACT OF AVARICE

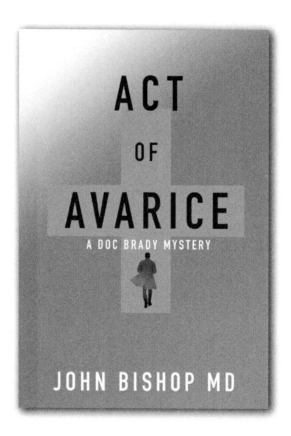

I hope you have enjoyed *Act of Mercy,* the seventh book in the Doc Brady Mystery series. I'm pleased to present you with a sneak peek of *Act of Avarice,* the eighth book.

Please visit **JohnBishopAuthor.com** to learn more.

CHAPTER 1

THE ROLLS

I was standing in the pedestrian lane at the HEB in Marble Falls, Texas, waiting my turn to cross what some drivers must have been pretending was the Indy 500 raceway, considering how fast they were traveling. Finally, a nice gentleman waved across several of us who were waiting with our grocery carts, prompting honks from those behind him. He rolled down his window and gave them the universal salute with his middle finger and continued to wave more shoppers across the lane until there were no more in sight.

One has to be a little careful in Texas. Most everyone is carrying or concealing a weapon of some sort, and I have not seen any groceries yet that are worth dying for. I gave the man a wave, and he returned the gesture with a half salute. As I walked in front of his red Chevy pickup, I noted he wore a WWII cap. He was part of the Greatest Generation, according to Tom Brokaw, which meant that he probably shouldn't be driving, as he had to be in his nineties. But this is Texas, where you don't give up your guns or your car without a fight. My own mother had a valid driver's license until she passed away in her mid-nineties, which I discovered only by accident in going through her things after her death. I opened a letter from the Department of Motor Vehicles, which was allowing her to renew her driver's license by mail, by email, or in person, with no driving test or vision test required. Amazing. I pondered how many folks in their nineties with auditory and visual impairments and a pistol on the passenger seat were out there driving and creating havoc on the roads. The thought made me consider shopping for groceries online at a store with delivery service.

I'm not a very good shopper. I tend to wander around and try out the food samples. You can make a meal off the bite-sized morsels at the HEB. There were lines at every food station. I loved their small-sized hot dogs, especially with fresh hot mustard. There were also the miniature beef Wellington bites, which were out-of-sight delicious. So I would usually load up the cart with frozen versions of the sampled bits, along with Nacho Cheese Doritos, ice cream sandwiches, Cheez-Its, Jimmy Dean breakfast sandwiches with sausage and pepper jack cheese, and an array of other items that should be accompanied by a coupon for a cardiovascular exam. Mary Louise would ask upon my return home about the missing bottled water, paper towels, Kleenex tissues, and toilet paper, those items that were on my original mission list, but that had lost priority somewhere between the barbecued pork ribs and the canapes with smoked salmon.

Mary Louise knew better than to send me to the grocery store, but that day she had no choice. She had driven to Austin for a charity board meeting; for which cause, I had forgotten. It was a Friday, the day I take off from my orthopedic surgery job at Hill Country Medical Center and hit the links with my golf-junkie buddies. I normally make rounds on hospital inpatients in the early morning then head to one of the four courses we are privileged to be members of as part of our membership at Horseshoe Bay Golf Club. This morning it had been the Summit course, a Jack Nicklaus Signature design with outstanding vistas of the Hill

Country and Lake LBJ. Because of a dinner party we were having at the house, I had to decline libations after golf and attend to my shopping duties as a favor to my bride.

As I was loading the rear of my Chevy Tahoe with the day's shopping bounty, I noticed an ancient Rolls Royce across the aisle from my car. It was one of the models with the sloped rear end, four-door, and with an odd color combination, brown on the top and hood, with cheesy yellow sides and trunk. I loved the style of the car, but who in the world would choose those two colors? Most of the Rolls I had admired over the years were a combination of silver and burgundy. But brown and yellow?

As I was staring at the Rolls and pondering the colors, a tall, thin man with slicked-back silver hair and carrying a grocery sack walked up to the vehicle, opened it, and sat his shopping bag in the trunk. He sensed me staring and turned my way.

"That is some automobile," I said. "What year?"

"1958 Silver Cloud, left-hand drive. I inherited it from my grandfather some years ago. I loved that man more than life itself and have been unable to part with it. It's of course a service nightmare, and only worth around $35,000 now, but back in the day, can you imagine what a chick magnet this car was?"

I laughed at that. "I can't help but notice the way you are dressed. You match the car."

He had on yellow pants, a yellow shirt, a brownish-yellow corduroy jacket with elbow patches, and matching Western pointed-toe boots in a yellow tint.

"I only take her out once a week, usually Friday, sometimes Sunday, and I feel she deserves the respect of my trying to match her in color. That's the only time I wear this outfit. Probably seems silly to you, huh?"

"No sir, not at all. I had an old 1982 Mercedes Benz 300 Turbodiesel I drove for twenty years. I understand the attachment."

"Have a fine day," he said, closing the trunk and boarding the Rolls. I went back to my business of loading my sacks chock-full of great items to eat—all bad for you—and hoped that I had managed to gather the necessities Mary Louise needed to prepare appetizers and dinner for our guests.

I heard the crunch of metal against metal, turned back toward the aisle, and saw the vintage Rolls crushing its left rear fender into a huge black GMC Denali. I yelled in the direction of the driver, but his window was up and I couldn't see within. I strode over to the car and noticed the Rolls was still in reverse, pushing against the SUV. I knocked on the driver's window, with no result. I grabbed the driver's door handle and pulled, and I saw him slumped against the steering wheel.

"Are you okay? You've run into another vehicle across the aisle," I said, with some desperation. He didn't respond but was coughing severely, and he had a gray tinge to his face. I reached in front of the driver, managed to grab the gear shift, forced it back into neutral, and shut off the engine. As I gently pulled his shoulders back against the seat, I noticed his skin color was worsening, and he had spittle coming out of his partially open mouth. It appeared he was in the midst of a stroke, a seizure, or a coronary artery occlusion, commonly known as a heart attack. His carotid pulse was thready, so I pushed him down into the seat and started cardiac massage. I attempted mouth-to-mouth resuscitation, but his airway wasn't clear, due to froth coming out of his nose and mouth, and my attempt to initiate respirations failed.

I backed out of the car, dialed 911 on my cell phone, gave the operator the location, and went back to trying to revive the driver. Several other folks appeared, asking me questions to which there were no answers. I made an attempt to clear his airway with a grease-stained towel I found in his glove box, but to no avail, then returned to my resuscitation efforts.

It seemed like forever, but the EMTs arrived within ten minutes, and we three hoisted the dying man onto a gurney. The medics brought the device up to waist height, quickly intubated the driver, started an IV line, and ran a portable EKG.

"He's in ventricular fibrillation," one said. "Get the defibrillator."

The other EMT went back into the fire department emergency vehicle, brought out the requested device, told everyone to stay clear, and shocked the driver's heart. The patient jumped several inches off the gurney during the shocking procedure, after which the other EMT determined the patient was back in sinus rhythm.

"Thanks for your help," the EMT said to me. "You might have saved this man's life. What's your name?"

"Jim Bob Brady. I'm an orthopedic surgeon at Hill Country Medical Center."

"That's where we're headed, Doc. You might consider following us over there, in case the ER docs and the cardiologist have any questions for you."

With that, they loaded the unknown patient into the ambulance and, sirens screaming, headed out of the parking lot.

"Hey, did you see what happened? That guy wrecked my truck," said the GMC owner.

"All I know is that he and I were having a conversation about his Rolls, he gets in the car, starts backing up, doesn't stop, and his fender met your bumper guard, which looks to me to be way oversized and made out of stainless steel. I see a little paint damage at the contact point, but it looks to me like his vehicle fared much worse than yours."

"Well, it's not my fault. Somebody has to pay!"

"Well, if the driver survives, I'm sure he'll try and accommodate you. If he doesn't, well maybe you can find a lawyer around here who will represent you against a dead man."

I left that jackass behind, walked back into HEB, and found a HELP counter. I asked for store security. The clerk looked at me like I had arrived from another planet. There was a nameplate in front of her station that read "Christie."

"Store security. You have security cameras in the store. I notice them whenever I shop here. If you have cameras, you have security. How about a store manager, Christie?"

She smacked her gum and blew a giant bubble, making me wonder how in the world she got a job at the HELP counter. So far, she was anything but. Her hair was dyed green on one side, blond on the other, although I couldn't tell if the blond was dyed or natural. She had several piercings in both ears and a small ring in her left nostril. I thought it likely that all that metal was causing a conductivity problem in her frontal lobe.

"Christie? Store manager, please?"

"You're that doctor, aren't you?"

"Excuse me?"

"That doctor at the hospital who got involved with those missing women last year. Brady, right?"

"Yes, Christie, I'm Dr. Jim Brady. I don't see what that has to do with—"

She got up from her chair, walked around the counter, came right up to my face, and hugged me. "Thank you for what you did. For all of us who used to let our partners kick us around and do what they wanted. You gave us individual strength, and even more strength in numbers. You changed my life, Doc. You, and Doctor Buck, and Sister Mads." She hugged me so tight I couldn't take a deep breath.

Christie finally released me, went back to her chair, and paged Scott to the HELP desk.

Scott, the store manager, who looked barely old enough to shave, arrived shortly thereafter. I related the events in the parking lot and handed him the keys to the Rolls Royce.

"My advice is to call the Marble Falls Police Department and tell them what happened. They can follow up with the owner at the hospital, provided he survives. They will probably impound the vehicle, for no other reason than to keep it safe."

"Thank you, sir. I've not encountered a situation such as this before. I appreciate your advice."

Scott left for the parking lot, and I bid Christie adieu. I was reminded of a saying that we all need to remember: you can't judge a book by its cover.

ABOUT THE AUTHOR

Dr. **John Bishop** has led a triple life. This orthopedic surgeon and keyboard musician has combined two of his talents into a third, as the author of the beloved Doc Brady mystery series. Beyond applying his medical expertise at a relatable and comprehensible level, Dr. Bishop, through his fictional counterpart Doc Brady, also infuses his books with his love of not only Houston and Galveston, Texas, but especially with his love for his adored wife. Bishop's talented Doc Brady is confident yet humble; brilliant, yet a genuinely nice and funny guy who happens to have a knack for solving medical mysteries. Above all, he is the doctor who will cure you of your blues and boredom. Step into his world with the first five books of the series, and you'll be clamoring for more.